P.S. NOT IF YOU WERE THE LAST MAN ON EARTH

J. S. COOPER

Created with Vellum

BLURB

P.S. Not If You Were The Last Man on Earth

To my tentmate,

I'm only going to say this once. I'm not interested in you. I will not be sharing a sleeping bag with you. I will not be asking you to keep me warm with your 'hot body.' Who calls their own body hot, by the way? I will not be doing a belly dance for you in the middle of the night, and I definitely won't be making you hot chocolate. You'll be lucky if I even alert you if there's a bear sighting, so don't push your luck. I'm going to be 100% honest with you. I'm not interested and have no desire to see you again after this trip.

Yours Unsincerely,
    Susie

P.S. Not if you were the last man on earth!

They say no good deed goes unpunished, and they're undoubtedly correct.

I agreed to go on a camping trip with my best friend and her new boyfriend, Finn, but I never agreed to share a tent with Finn's best friend, Brody.

Brody is a pompous, full-of-himself jock. He thinks he rules the world because he's some hotshot baseball player, but the joke's on him, as I don't even watch sports. I just need to get past this weekend without killing him, and then I never have to deal with his arrogant ass again.

ONE
SUSIE

A loud cracking sound from about two feet away from me made me doubt my sanity. My head snapped to the right, and my eyes narrowed as I peered through the dense brush of the trees. I couldn't see what had made the noise, but I wasn't happy.

I wasn't happy at all.

"What was that?" I asked no one in particular. My best friend, Marcia, was pressed against a tree, kissing her new boyfriend, Finn, and while I was happy for her, I couldn't stop myself from rolling my eyes. I wanted to shout, "Get a room," but there was no room to get.

"Just a bear." The humor in Brody's voice irritated me. "Hopefully, it won't come into your tent and eat you tonight." He growled and waved his arms around him, and I pressed my lips together. "You don't want the big, bad bear to eat you up."

"Well, if it does, then you'll be next," I snapped as I stared at the man next to me. "You're in the same tent."

"Don't sound so happy about it, Susie."

"Oh, can't you tell? I'm ecstatic."

"I'm glad to hear that." Brody smirked, and I just stared at him. He was one of Finn's best friends, and we had not hit it off. In fact, I'd only met him once before this trip, and that had been one time too many. I knew men like him—handsome, rich, cocky—but I refused to let him get under my skin.

"We should put up said tent now, though." He nodded to the open ground next to the trees. "We want to do it before it gets dark."

"I cannot believe this is my life." I sighed, looking out over the dirt completely surrounded by a thick expanse of trees before turning back at him. "All I wanted was an all-expenses-paid trip to Barbados or Hawaii. Shit, I even would have settled for Las Vegas—a nice luxurious suite with a big bath to soak in. But no, I get this."

"I know." He unzipped his backpack. "Aren't you lucky?"

"So lucky," I dragged out. A bee buzzed past me, and I jumped back. I stared at the bags dumped on the ground a few feet away from us and wondered if I would make it through this weekend without bursting into tears. I'd always dreamed of visiting California, but I'd hoped to be sipping martini's on the beach, not flicking bugs off lukewarm water bottles.

"Do you know how many women would die to be in your position?" He raised an eyebrow, looking self-assured.

"Oh?" I said softly, stepping closer to him. I licked my lips and ran my hands through my long, dark hair. "Do you think so?"

He grinned as he stared at my lips. "I know so. Women would do anything to..." His eyes widened as I took another step closer to him and raised my head toward his. I knew he thought I was going to kiss him. I knew he thought I'd all of a sudden fallen under his spell.

"Do this?" I said as I pushed him back into a bunch of dry leaves. I laughed as I looked down at him as he blinked up at me. "You might think you're a big shot, Brody Wainwright, but in my world, you are a nothing."

"Tell me what you really think, Susie." He jumped up and brushed the autumn leaves off his jeans. "If you wanted to get your hands on me, you could have just asked."

"I didn't want to get my hands on you." I glared at him. "Trust me. You're the last man on earth I would ever want to get my hands on." I stared at his handsome face and knew that wasn't quite true, but he didn't need to know that.

"Really?" He blinked at me several times, his mouth open in surprise as if no woman had ever muttered such a thing to him before. "So I guess it all ends with us."

"What all ends with us?"

"Humanity."

"What are you talking about?"

"If I was the last man on earth and you were the last woman, and you turned me down, then there would be no more children, and thus, the end of the world. How does that make you feel, Susie? You are solely responsible for the end of the world." He held his hands up to the universe, and I couldn't stop myself from ogling his muscles. I made sure not to stare too long, but Brody was cut.

"God, give me patience. Please!" I turned my back on him and gasped as I heard more cracking branches from the trees. My heart raced as I snuck a glance back at Brody, who was staring at me with a smile on his face. "Come on, let's put this tent up."

"Yes, ma'am." He bowed and then turned around. "Hey,

lovebirds, we're going to put up the tents now. Are you going to join us?"

"Coming," Finn called back and pulled away from a giggling Marcia. He grabbed her hand and gave her a loving smile. My heart ached slightly as she beamed at him.

I'd never seen my best friend so happy. None of her other boyfriends had ever made her beam like he did. It was like he'd found a light switch inside of her that had never been turned on before. It was amazing to me to see how light and happy and carefree she was around him. Marcia had always had a tenseness to her when she was around her ex-boyfriends. And while I'd liked some of her exes, I'd never loved any of them. None of them had been the right fit.

But Finn... well, Finn was her other half. Finn made me believe that maybe soul mates did exist after all, because he and Marcia were quite obviously made for each other.

"Sickening, isn't it?" Brody interrupted my thoughts as he gazed at Finn and Marcia.

"I think it's quite lovely, actually."

"Oh, you're one of those."

"One of what?" I wanted to bite down on my tongue for falling for his bait.

"A true romantic." The way he said the words, you would have thought he was talking about being a serial killer.

"Why? Because I believe in love?" I could hear the tension in my raising voice. This man knew how to trigger and annoy me, and I was letting him rile me up. I needed to learn how to ignore him.

"Lust is not love."

"Did I say it was?" I sighed. "You think you know me, Brody, but I'm not like every other bimbo you've met."

"So you're a unique bimbo?" His eyes twinkled with laughter. He was clearly loving this conversation. Brody was obviously the sort of man that liked to get on women's nerves. I was pretty sure he would keep trying to irritate me if I kept responding the way I was.

"Excuse me?" I glared at him. "How dare you call me a bimbo."

"Actually, I didn't. You called yourself one. You said you're not like the other bimbos I've met, thus putting yourself in that group."

"Let's just put this tent up." I shook my head as I took in the pile of canvas and poles. I bent down and picked up what appeared to be the frame and started to unfold it. "Some help, please?"

"Of course." He nodded and grabbed part of the frame. His fingers grazed mine for a brief second, and a jolt of electricity coursed through me. Our eyes met, and I waited for him to say something snide, but he didn't. He narrowed his green eyes for a few seconds, and then his face relaxed. "So, how do you know Marcia?"

"We grew up together in Florida. We've been best friends since we were kids. We went to elementary, high school, and college together. Honestly, she's more like my sister than my friend."

He pushed some stakes into the ground. "Have you ever had a falling out?"

"We've always been best friends. Well, there was this one time when we didn't speak for two weeks." I wanted to ask him why he cared. It was so odd for him to want to know if we'd ever had a falling out, but I didn't really want to engage too much with him. No matter that his piercing gaze made my insides turn to mush.

"Oh, what happened?"

"Do not tell him." Marcia laughed as she approached us. "I don't want him to think poorly of me."

"You slept with her boyfriend?" Brody's eyes widened, and he grinned wickedly. "How scandalous." He rubbed his hands together like some sort of salacious old maid, and I couldn't stop myself from laughing.

"No, nothing like that," I said. "You watch too much TV."

"I don't watch any TV, actually," he said. "I watch sports, but that's for work."

"Okay then." Boring. I didn't want to tell him that I loved TV shows. I knew I watched far too much of it, and I didn't want him judging me. Especially if he were to ask which shows I watched. I definitely kept a lot of trashy TV shows on the air.

"I make Finn watch TV with me," Marcia interjected as Finn gathered the canvas for their tent. "Though he falls asleep whenever I put on a reality show."

"Reality TV is for the dogs." Finn shook his head. "I've never seen anything so inane in my life."

"What about when Barbie and Tanya argued about that dress in college?" Brody grinned, and Finn started laughing.

"Okay, maybe that was inane."

"Barbie and Tanya?" Marcia raised an eyebrow and looked over at Finn. I could tell she was slightly jealous by the way she wrinkled her brow and rubbed her palms on her pants. "Who are they?" Her voice was far too nonchalant to be believable.

"Two sorority girls we knew in college." Finn chuckled. "All they ever did was talk about clothes."

"And one night, they came over wearing the same dress," Brody added. "And they spent the whole evening arguing over who should change. I was like, 'Take it off and let's get busy. That's why you came over anyway.'" He pursed his lips and gyrated his hips like he was in a club.

I looked at him in disgust. "You really are a pig, aren't you?"

"I don't oink. But I guess if you wanted me to do it in the bedroom, I could." He winked at me. Did this guy take nothing seriously?

"Hey, Susie Q. Shall we let the guys put up the tents while we go for a walk?" Marcia grabbed my arm and smiled. I knew she could read me well enough to know that my pressed lips and vacant eyes meant I was about to go off on Brody. I tapped my fingers together and exhaled. I was never good at breathing techniques, and I hated yoga, but I always knew to exhale when I was starting to get mad. It had stopped me from saying things I would regret several times.

"Yeah, let's do that." I nodded as I dropped the tent. I followed behind her out of our campsite and to the main road.

"I'm going to kill that guy," I growled as soon as we were out of earshot.

"I'm sorry, Susie. He's not that bad, is he?" Marcia looked at me hopefully. "And he's so cute."

"He's not bad looking, but he knows it."

"Not bad?" She laughed. "Girl, Brody Wainwright is absolutely gorgeous."

"Then you share a tent with him." I pursed my lips together. "This is not the trip I thought it was going to be."

"Are you mad at me?" I could tell from the look on her face that she was genuinely worried. I also knew from our years' long friendship that she was out of her comfort zone as well. Neither one of us was really into the great outdoors.

"No, I'm happy that you're happy." I squeezed her

hand. "You and Finn really seem to have an amazing connection." They had the sort of connection I hoped to find with a man. And I was so happy that she had found that with someone because I knew the crappy guys she'd dated before had made her feel like nothing. Finn loved and worshipped her, and I'd never seen her happier in my life.

"He's perfect." She paused. "Well, maybe he's not perfect, but he's perfect for me." She beamed and played with the small silver ring he'd given her. She wore it on her pinky finger, and I knew she loved that ring more than any other jewelry she owned.

"You're literally glowing."

"He does make my heart glow. I know that sounds cheesy, and I'm the last person in the world to be cheesy, but he's the fire to my fireplace."

"Oh, Marcia." I groaned. "That is past cheesy." I glanced at the path ahead of us and the trees in front of us. It really was beautiful here. "Yosemite here we are. Make a believer out of us."

"Who would have thought we'd be camping in a national park?" Marcia asked, and I shook my head.

"Not me." A waterfall sounded from the distance, and the warbling of a Steller's Jay filled my ears. I smiled to myself as we continued walking, taking some deep breaths and enjoying the cool air as it filled my lungs. The smell of cedar and fir trees filled my nostrils. I wished I had a way to bottle it up and take it home with me. It wasn't so bad being out here in nature, but that was a thought I'd keep to myself.

TWO
BRODY

"So what's Susie's story?" I asked Finn as we worked at getting the campsite ready before the girls got back. "She seems like she has a stick in her ass or something."

He grinned as he shook out the sleeping bags. "She's just a little bit reserved."

"A little bit reserved? She's colder than an iceberg." I shivered. "Did we go to Antarctica or California?"

"No, she's not cold. You're so dramatic, Brody."

"Trust me, she is. I'd get more softness out of a hedgehog."

"Just because she doesn't want you doesn't mean she's hard."

"Oh, Finn. We both know she wants me." I shrugged as he rolled his eyes. "I'm just wondering if I should hook up with her, if and when she sneaks into my sleeping bag." My eyes narrowed as Finn started laughing. "What's so funny?"

"Dude, do you hear yourself? Susie is not interested in you."

"She's playing hard to get." The words sounded arrogant, even to my own ears, but I couldn't stop myself. Susie had intrigued me from the first moment I'd seen her. Her face was earnest and pretty, her eyes alert and all-seeing, and her lips were lush and delectable. She was the sort of woman I'd love to bed and then run fast away from. She was too dangerous for a man like me.

"I don't think she's playing anything." He handed me two sleeping bags. "Put these into your tent." I grabbed them, unzipped my tent, and placed the sleeping bags on the floor. "Be nice to her. She's Marcia's best friend, and I can't afford for her to not like me."

"So you're really serious about Marcia?"

"I love her. I'm going to marry her one day, so I'd say so." He nodded and gave me a look. "Do not mess around with Susie. Be on your best behavior."

"I'm not looking to mess around with her." I grinned. "I'm just having some fun teasing her. She's pretty." Pretty was an understatement. Susie was gorgeous. Even the way she glared at me turned me on.

"She's not your type."

"What does that mean?" I was starting to take his words as a challenge. Why was he so determined for her not to like me?

"She's not a groupie. She's not—"

"I take offense to that. I do date women that aren't groupies." That was technically true, though most of the women I met and hooked up with were excited at the possibility of being with a baseball star.

"You don't date anyone." He gave me a pointed look. "They don't call you the player of baseball for no reason."

"Don't be a player hater."

"I'm not." He cleared his throat. "Brody, you know I love you, but do not fuck around with Susie, okay?"

"Okay." I nodded as I stared at my best friend. "You really love, Marcia, huh?"

"I do."

I was about to quip back a funny retort, but I thought better of it. I'd never seen Finn like this before. We'd met our freshman year of college when we'd both walked on to the baseball team. He was one of my longest friendships, aside from a few high school friends that I didn't really keep in contact with. He knew me as well as anyone did, and he could tell there was something beyond the façade I put on. Though, I was grateful he didn't try and push anything. We were men. We didn't have to talk about our feelings.

"No worries, bro." I ran my hands through my hair. "I won't fuck her. I can keep it zipped up until we get back to New York. Did I tell you about this hot Latina chick I met at the club last week? Eva was her name. She had a bangin' body. Long black hair. Dark eyes. Deep red lips that looked like they could suck a cock for hours. She can call me Papi, anytime."

"You're an idiot. You know that, right?"

"You're just mad that you're down to one pussy." I chuckled. There was a hollowness to my laugh, and I wondered if he noticed. I would never admit it to Finn, but I was slightly taken aback and jealous of the fact that he'd settled down and seemed so domesticated. I just couldn't see that for myself. When you were with one woman, you had to share too much of your life. And that was something I wasn't willing to do.

"Let's get a fire started, Brody."

"Yes, captain." I looked around for the firepit. "You brought wood?"

"Yeah, I picked some up at the gas station." He walked over to the truck, opened the back door, and started pulling out some bags. I headed over to help him, and I was suddenly hit with memories from my childhood, hanging out with my two brothers.

"Brody, grab the axe." My older brother, Michael, had called back to me as we'd walked out of the barn on our grandparents' farm in Kentucky. I'd grabbed it and held it gingerly, nervous it would hit me in the leg. I'd only been ten—a tall, gangly kid with long limbs and zero coordination.

"You're not carrying it right." My younger brother, Patrick, had grabbed the axe from me and carried it like he was a woodsman.

"Come on, guys." Michael had run ahead of us. "We need to cut down some trees for Gramps and Grams."

"Coming." Patrick had stupidly run too. If our parents had been there, he never would have gone running with an axe in his hands.

"Hey, Brody. You in la-la land?" Finn frowned as he hit me in the shoulder.

"Sorry, what?"

"I asked if you had a lighter." He nodded toward the firepit.

"Nah, man. Sorry. You don't have one?"

"Somewhere." He went to his truck, and I checked my phone. I had fifty missed calls from about six different women and my manager. I scrolled through the texts to see if there was anything important, though there never was. I opened a few of the photos sent to me—some topless shots, and one woman had decided to show me what she could do with a ping-pong ball. I tilted my head to the side to get a better look and laughed to myself.

"What's so funny?" Finn asked as he headed back toward me. "What are you looking at?"

"Your little old lady wouldn't want you to see what I'm looking at, bro."

"What?" He stared at the phone and then back at me. "Don't tell me, titties and things?"

"Things. And titties, of course."

"You don't ever get bored of looking at that shit, Brody?"

"Did you?" I raised an eyebrow at him. Was Finn trying to rewrite history here? He was at the strip club alongside me more often than not before he met Marcia. Shit, I could remember one night in Vegas when his hotel room became the strip club.

"Heh, maybe not. But that shit did get old. You couldn't have a conversation with any of those women without worrying you'd find yourself on TMZ the next day."

"True." I nodded. "Darryl found that out the hard way."

"Yup. Ten million hard ways."

"Yeah, well. I'm not stupid." I powered my phone off and put it into my back pocket. "I'm here to relax this weekend. Refresh my mind, and all that new-age shit."

"Brody, you need to relax. Just let your guard down. Susie is good people. Enjoy her company."

"I'd love to enjoy her company." I winked at him. "I can keep her warm at night."

"She's not that type of girl." He shook his head. "Don't fuck around with her."

"I won't fuck her unless she begs me, but then the begging might keep you and Marcia up." I grinned at him, and he sighed.

"Brody, just be serious for once, okay? This is important to me. Marcia and Susie are important to me. I know you like to pretend like everything is all fun and games, but bro, I know you. The guard can come down a little bit. We're all friends here. You can just be yourself."

"I am being myself." Out of all my friends, Finn was the one that knew me the best. He didn't know all of me, but he saw the man that very few people got to. He saw the Brody that my family had known growing up.

The one I tried to hide. The one I never wanted to be again.

THREE

SUSIE

"That was absolutely delicious." Marcia looked over at Finn with a loving smile on her face. "I didn't know you could cook like that."

"You know I'm a pretty dab hand with a grill." He grinned. "I just haven't been able to show you because we live in New York. But if we were to move to..."

"Finn." She glared at him, and he chuckled.

"What? I've got to try and convince you somehow."

"What are you talking about?" I said, looking at them in confusion.

"Finn doesn't want to live in New York City," Marcia said with a shrug.

"Well, look around you," Finn said, staring at the stars in the sky. "Do you see the stars in Manhattan? Do you see the moon? Do you hear the sounds of the birds at night? The rustling of the trees? Are you a hundred feet from a mountain?"

"But that's why we moved to the city," I said. "Because we liked the hustle and bustle. We grew up in a small town in Florida, and we wanted something new."

"You didn't have mountains in Florida, though, did you?" Finn said with a smile.

"No, but we weren't looking for mountains." I narrowed my eyes at Marcia. "Are you moving to California? Is that why you wanted me to come on this trip?"

"We're not moving to California. I promise you."

"Really, Marcia?" Finn looked surprised. "I thought you said you'd think about it."

She sighed. "One day, maybe. But I literally just moved to New York. And you know I want to experience life there."

"Uh-oh," Brody said. "Look what you've done, Susie."

"What have I done?"

"You've caused a fight between the lovebirds."

"I haven't caused any fight. I'm just curious, because it was Marcia that convinced me to move to New York City with her, even though I wasn't quite ready, and she's the one with the job. And now she has a boyfriend and wants to leave? I'm just trying to figure out where I stand here."

"That's not what's happening," Marcia said. "You know that, right?"

"I'm just trying to figure out—"

"We're not leaving Manhattan anytime soon." Finn walked over to me and put his arm around my shoulder. "You've been a really great friend to Marcia. I know how much she depends on you, and I know how much your friendship means to her. And yes, I don't want to live the rest of my life in the city, but we're not moving now. I didn't want to get you upset."

I stared at his handsome face and then looked over at Marcia.

I understood. I understood now why she'd fallen in love with him. He was a kind man, a good person, and I was appreciative of the fact that he'd come over to comfort me.

"Thanks," I said. "It's not like I can't be by myself, but I just thought I'd get to spend some time in the city with my best friend, especially now that she has a job and can take me everywhere."

"What is it that you do again, Marcia?" Brody asked, and Marcia and I both started laughing. "Can I know what the laughter's about?" Brody looked at each one of us in turn. "I'm in the dark here."

"Marcia works for Finn at his company," I said. "I can't believe you didn't know that." I hoped my voice didn't belie the fact that I was envious that my best friend was dating the CEO of a corporation. It wasn't that I even cared about money that much, but it certainly made it easier and less stressful to not have to worry how one would pay their rent each month.

"Finn doesn't tell me about all his employees. Okay then. So it was an office romance?"

"Something like that," Finn replied.

"And what is it that you do, Susie?" Brody continued.

"I'm actually about to start a job soon."

"Oh yeah," Marcia said. "So you've decided on which position you're going to take?" I stared at her, my eyes a little wide, hoping she wasn't going to continue.

I hadn't exactly told Marcia what my new job was. I'd been offered a position as a telephone psychic, but my conscience hadn't let me take that. Too many people were gullible, and I'd hate to think that anyone acted upon my words. Instead, I'd accepted another position because rent was due. And now that Marcia was dating Finn, I didn't want either one of them to think that I wasn't going to pull my own weight. I didn't want them to think that just because Finn was loaded that I expected him to pay all of our rent. I was going to find my half come hell or high water.

"Come on now. What's this job?" Brody said, his eyes narrowing. "I'm curious."

"I don't really want to talk about it right now. Shall we go look at the stars or something?"

"You can see the stars right here," Brody said dryly. "It seems to me that you don't want to tell us."

"I have no problem telling you guys, but no one wants to hear about my boring job."

"I want to know," Finn said, and I glared at him. "Or maybe I don't," he said quickly. "If you don't want to tell us about it, that's fine."

"I mean, I'd rather..."

"What, are you going to be some sort of stripper?" Brody said with a laugh. "If you want to practice on me right now, you can. I don't have a lot of singles, but I promise you I'm good for it."

"No, I'm not going to be a stripper." I couldn't believe the gall of this guy to make assumptions and comments as he did.

"What? I think you'd make a pretty sexy stripper. Your personality won't be winning any awards, but maybe you don't have to talk at the strip club."

"My personality is absolutely wonderful, thank you very much."

"I don't know," he said. "I'd be scared that you'd bite my head off while you were dancing on my lap."

"Excuse me?" I stared at him.

"What? I didn't stutter."

I rolled my eyes.

"What? It's true. You'd be on my lap grinding, and I'd

be scared you'd..." He paused as Finn glared at him. "Okay, sorry. I was just joking."

"I don't know what it is about you two. You're like children," Finn said, shaking his head.

Marcia laughed. "And Susie says I'm the combative one."

"I'm not being combative. It's him. He's the one that's always picking on me. So anything I have to say, he's got something to say in return. He's just rude."

"What? I asked you what your job is. I'm trying to get to know you. I care about your life. Is that so bad?" He held his hands up in the air and then jumped up. "I don't know. Every other woman I've met has been delighted to tell me what they do for a living. I'm just being nice. I really don't care what you do, Susie Q."

"Don't call me that."

"Don't call you what?" He grinned. "Susie Q?"

"Yeah."

"Why not? You don't like it?"

"You don't know me well enough to call me that. Only my best friends call me Susie Q."

"What if I just call you Q instead?"

"No, you're not going to call me Q. What if I just called you Y?"

"Y?" He stared at me in confusion.

"Brody ends with a Y."

"Yeah, but it doesn't rhyme." He chuckled and shook his head. "Nice try, Susie, but you didn't quite get there."

"Um, Brody, you do realize that Susie Q doesn't rhyme either?" I wanted to add *dumbass* to the end of that, but I knew I had to be nice, or Marcia would think I was deliberately trying to antagonize him.

"Oh my gosh, guys." Marcia jumped up as well. "Is this what you two are going to be like all weekend?"

"Well, you should've told me this guy was coming, or you should've gotten me a separate tent."

"You wouldn't want to sleep in a tent by yourself. You know that, Susie."

"I'd be fine."

"Really? What if a bear came in the middle of the night?"

"It's not like he's going to protect me." I pointed at Brody.

"Would you want me to protect you?" He walked over to me and held his arms out. "If you want to come running into my arms, I'll have them open at any time."

"I will not be running into your arms."

"You can come sit on my lap instead." He winked.

"I am not one of your fans, and I'm not a groupie. So save it, Brody Wainwright."

"I like it when you say my name," he said with a smirk. "I really do."

"I'm sure."

"So, are you going to tell us what you do or..."

I sighed. "Fine. Do you really want to know what my new job is?"

"Yeah, I kind of do."

Finn nodded as well. "I can't lie, Susie. I'm curious as well."

Marcia grinned. "Well, you know I want to know. What is it?"

"Fine. It's going to be on the phone."

"Yeah?" Finn prodded me.

"Somewhat of a customer service role."

"Oh," Marcia said. "For who? Like a bank?"

"Not a bank. But I guess... businessmen."

"What sort of customer service role is there for businessmen?" Finn said, confused. "Are you going to work for American Express?"

"That would be a bank, silly." Marcia grabbed his hand.

"You're right. I wasn't thinking."

"Let me think," Brody said. "Customer service on the phone for businessmen. Are you going to work for an airline?"

"No."

"Are you going to work for a concierge service?"

"No. I doubt you'll be able to guess it."

"It's something you didn't want to tell us, so obviously, it's not necessarily on the up and up."

"What does that mean?"

"It's obvious that you're not doing customer service for the FBI or the CIA, or you would've been excited to tell us that. So there's got to be something that embarrasses you, or something you're not quite happy about with this job. Maybe you're even ashamed of it?"

"I'm not ashamed of it. A job is a job," I said, glaring at him. He was getting far too close for comfort. "Anyway, are we going to go and look at the stars or..."

"Oh no, I'd much rather play this game," Brody said.

"Yeah," Finn said. "And I want to show Marcia something, so maybe we can do the walk later?"

"Okay, well, fine. If everyone just wants to—"

"Oh, no, no, no," Finn said. "I can show Marcia after you tell us what the job is."

"Fine. Oh my gosh! I'm going to be a phone sex operator." I almost shouted it and then closed my mouth. Marcia's eyes widened, and I could see Finn laughing as he stared at Brody.

"Okay," Finn said. "I don't really know what to say to that."

"And you said stripper was a rude suggestion?" Brody threw his head back. "Dude, how in the world is a phone sex operator any better than a stripper?"

"Because I'm not going to be having sex or touching anyone," I said.

He grinned at me. "Yeah, but you're going to be getting guys off."

"You're disgusting."

"I'm disgusting? Honey, do you know what your job is?"

"I haven't started yet."

"Guys are going to be calling you to whack off, okay? In the strip club, guys can't openly whack off. Some might try, or a stripper might do it for them, but they're not going to be whacking off to your voice. Whereas when..."

"Okay, I get it. Thank you very much."

"They're lucky, though," he said softly.

"What does that mean?"

"You're gorgeous and you have a nice voice. So"—he shrugged—"I wouldn't mind having phone sex with you."

"Okay, conversation over." I glared at him and then looked over to Marcia. "You owe me big time."

"I really do." She nodded and then looked at Finn.

Finn cleared his throat. "Hey, Susie."

"Yeah?"

"I know you previously said you're not interested because you don't believe in nepotism, but the offer still stands. If you want to work at—"

"No," I cut him off. "You are my best friend's boyfriend, and while I appreciate the offer, I'm not going to take advantage of your relationship or our friendship."

"But you have the qualifications," Marcia said quickly.

"You have more qualifications than me. You had a better GPA. You..."

"I don't want to take advantage of this situation, okay? I'll just do what I got to do."

"And that's being a phone sex operator?" Brody raised an eyebrow.

"It's not that I *want* to be a phone sex operator. I'm actually looking for a position as a substitute teacher, but I don't have the certifications and..." I sighed. "Anyway, long story."

"Is that what you want to do with your life?" he asked softly. "You want to be a teacher?"

"I don't know," I replied.

"You'll figure it out," Finn said with a smile. "I have faith in you."

"Thanks, Finn," I said.

Marcia gave him a big kiss on the cheek, and they stared at each other adoringly.

"Go on, guys," I told them. "Go and do whatever you want to do. I'll see you both in the morning, okay?"

"Night, Susie." Marcia walked over to me and gave me a big hug. "I love you."

"Love you too," I said and kissed her on the cheek. "Night, Finn."

"Night, Suze." He grinned. "Night, Brody."

"Night, man. Don't do anything I wouldn't do." Brody chuckled. "But then, I guess that's not much."

Marcia shook her head, and we watched the two of them walk out of the campsite. I had no idea where they were going, but most probably, Finn had some romantic spot to show her.

"So I guess it's just you and me," Brody said.

I groaned. "I think I'm going to go to bed."

"It's eight o'clock."

"Yeah. So?"

"You're going to go to bed at eight o'clock?"

"Well, yeah."

"We could go look at the stars," he said.

"I don't think so. I think I'm going to get into my bed."

"You mean your sleeping bag?" He laughed.

"Yeah, that's what I mean."

"Look, Susie. I know we got off to a bit of a rough start, and my teasing you hasn't helped, but we're going to be spending the entire weekend together. You know the love-birds aren't going to have that much time for us, so if we want to enjoy the weekend, which I know I do, maybe we can start afresh?"

"You and me, start afresh?"

"Just for the weekend. Then you can go back to hating me when we get back to New York."

"Let me think about it."

"Come on. I know a really cool hike," he said. "It's not far, and we can see the sky, and I can show you a whole bunch of constellations. Maybe we'll even see some owls."

"You think so?" I said softly. "I've always wanted to see an owl in real life."

"I can't make any promises, but maybe." His face was animated and alive. He looked around, paying keen attention to the tree branches, and I could tell this was something that really excited him.

"How do you know so much about nature anyway?" I said.

"Why? I can't know about nature just because I'm a baseball player?"

"I don't know. You do seem like a player."

"I lived in Kentucky every summer for years," he said softly.

"Every summer?"

"My grandparents—they had a farm there, and my parents would send me and my brothers." His voice trailed off. "But enough about me. Shall we go for a walk, or are you going to go mope in the bed?"

"Fine. We can go," I said. "Let me just grab a jacket, okay? It's getting cool."

"Okay." He nodded. "And maybe..."

"Yeah?" I asked him as he paused.

"Maybe you can tell me your best phone-sex lines."

"Oh my gosh. Really, Brody?"

"What? A man's got to try. Because who knows? Maybe you would've agreed," he said in a deep, husky voice, and I couldn't stop myself from laughing.

"You're a goof, Brody Wainwright."

"Look at that," he said, his eyes crinkling. "I made you laugh. Never thought I'd see the day. You're already warming to me."

"Don't count your chickens before they hatch," I said, shaking my head. "You're an idiot and a pig and a—"

"I know." He held his hands up. "Every bad word you can think of. But for the rest of the weekend, why can't I just be the charming guy you're sharing your tent with?"

"Fine," I said. "Only for the rest of the weekend, though."

FOUR

BRODY

Susie and I walked in companionable silence as we made our way toward Vernal Falls. I knew Yosemite quite well. I'd been here a couple of times when I was a teenager and had never forgotten those trips with my family.

I wanted to ask Susie about her phone-sex job and tease her, but I knew she was quite sensitive about the subject. In fact, she seemed almost too sensitive to be successful in that profession. If she got offended at me teasing her and asking these questions, I couldn't imagine how she would feel when dirty men got on the phone wanting her to role-play and act out their various kinks. She didn't seem like that sort of woman, and I wanted to know why she'd taken such a job, especially when her best friend was dating Finn, and he'd offered her a job.

Finn was a billionaire. He could afford to pay her whatever she wanted. And from all accounts, it seemed she had a great degree. I could tell by the way she spoke that she was intelligent. Ultimately, I knew she didn't know me well enough or trust me enough to tell me why she'd taken such a job.

"Are you tired?" I asked her, noticing she'd slowed down as we were walking.

"A bit. I haven't really hiked in a long time. And if I'm honest, I've never really been much of a hiker, so I'm kind of out of shape."

"You don't look like you're out of shape." I smiled as I looked over her womanly figure.

She was filled out in all the right places. She had big boobs, which I had a pension for, and a large ass, though she wasn't overweight. I couldn't lie. She looked like she'd be dynamite in bed, but that wasn't something I was going to tell her.

She played with her long black hair and yawned slightly.

"We don't have to hike all the way there, then," I said. "It's a lot for one day, I know."

"But you said you wanted to. I don't mind."

"Wow, you're being nice to me," I said, feigning shock.

"Don't get used to it." She grinned.

"Oh, I don't think I could. I doubt it'll last much longer."

"Yeah, well, not if you say something that annoys me."

"It seems like almost everything I say annoys you."

"Not when you're being normal."

"I thought I was always being normal."

"No. Sometimes you're a cocky bastard."

"Really? You think I'm a cocky bastard?"

"Yeah, and I bet I'm not the only woman that's ever said that."

I started laughing. She was right, of course. I'd been called an asshole and a bastard so many times that I almost felt as though those terms were my nicknames.

"So, Brody."

"Yes, Susie."

"Tell me more about you."

"What do you want to know?"

"Did you always want to be a baseball player?"

I looked at her in surprise. My nostrils flared as I took a deep breath. She was staring at me with an inquisitive expression. I wasn't sure how to answer her because no one had ever asked me that. Most people just assumed that I'd always wanted to be a baseball player, but that was far from the truth. "No," I said. "I didn't."

"Oh, okay. But you were just good at it or..." She paused for a moment. "I don't mean to pry. It's okay if you don't want to talk about it."

"You're not prying," I said. "I didn't actually play sports when I was in high school. I was a bit of a nerd." I said the words lightly, but I flinched as it registered that I'd said them out loud.

"Oh, really? You were a nerd? You don't look like it."

I nodded in agreement. "I know I don't."

"So are you going to tell me more? I'm surprised you didn't play in high school. Did you play in college?"

"I did play in college, yeah."

She stared at me for a few seconds, and I stared back at her. I wasn't used to having these kinds of conversations with people. Men thought I was cool because I was a professional baseball player, and women thought I was cool because I was hot and a professional baseball player. No one had ever asked me about why I got into the sport, or when, and I didn't know how I felt about that.

"If you don't want to tell me—"

"No, it's just... It's unusual for someone to ask me questions like this."

"I'm just asking you a regular question, no?"

"I guess most women want to know the amount of money I have in my bank account or where I'm going to take them shopping. They don't really ask me about myself. Maybe they ask if I'm looking for a girlfriend or a wife or if I want to have kids or something like that, but not about me."

"Then you're really dating the wrong sort of women," she said softly, "because any woman that was trying to get to know you would want to know about *you*."

"Are you trying to get to know me?"

"Yeah. That's why I'm asking you the questions."

"So do you consider this a date?"

"Are you joking, Brody?" She stared at me and shook her head. "You're joking, right?"

"I don't know. I'm asking you a question."

"No, I'm not trying to date you. How many times do I have to tell you that?"

"I'm just checking. I mean—"

"I know, I know. You're Brody Wainwright. You're a top baseball player for the New York Yankees, and you're handsome and rich and blah, blah, blah. I'm going to fill you in on something."

"Yeah?"

"I don't watch baseball. I don't care about baseball. I don't care how much money you have. I don't care that you play for the Yankees. I couldn't care less if you were from fricking Mars, okay?"

"Well, I'm not from Mars."

"I know. You're from Kentucky."

"Actually, I'm not from Kentucky. I grew up in Pennsylvania, and my grandparents lived in Kentucky."

"Did you grow up in Philly?" she asked me.

"No. I actually grew up in a small town in northern Pennsylvania."

"Okay. I don't know Pennsylvania that well, or I'd ask you the name of the town."

"Yeah, most people wouldn't have heard of my town."

"So you grew up in a small town in Pennsylvania. Did you have a large family?"

"I was a middle child. Two brothers."

"So there's three of you. Any sisters?"

"No."

"And you visited your grandparents in Kentucky. Are you a country boy or something?" She started laughing, and I smiled at her, though the insides of my stomach started curling. I flashed back to my sophomore year of high school.

"Hey there, Wainwright," one of the football players had called me out as I was walking down the hallway with my biology textbook.

"Hi," I'd said.

"What are you doing, nerd?"

"Excuse me?"

"I said what are you doing, nerd? I can't believe you're a Wainwright."

"I don't know how to answer that." I had stared at him. And then a bunch of girls had started laughing. The football player had been about to say something else when my older brother came out of one of the classrooms and saw that I was being picked on.

"Hey, what's going on?" He'd walked over to the football player, who was one of his best friends. They'd been on the team together, and my brother Michael had actually been the quarterback of the team.

"I was just saying that your brother is a lame-o. Biology over sports?"

"Dude, leave him alone."

"I just don't get at it. How is he such a hick when you guys are—"

"How am I a hick just because I'm studious?" I'd asked him. "Piss off."

"You're a hick because you'd rather spend time on the farm than hang out."

I'd pressed my lips together, close to tears. I couldn't believe my brother wasn't sticking up for me more.

"Dude, just leave him alone," Michael had said. "Come on, let's go throw some ball." And they'd walked off.

I'd known I was different. In a school that had valued sports and dating and getting laid, I'd been the nerd, and I stuck out like a sore thumb being a Wainwright. No girls had wanted me, with my bad acne and braces, and I'd started going to help my grandparents on the farm during the summer because they hadn't been able to afford the help they'd needed to keep the farm going. This had stopped me from going to parties and bonding with my brother's friends, and I was a bit of a loner.

"Hey, Brody." Susie's hand grazed my arm, and I looked at her, blinking. "You okay there?"

"Yeah, I'm fine. Why?"

"You were just saying something about the fact that you're not a hick, and I just wanted to say that I didn't mean to offend you if..."

"No, no, I'm not offended. Of course not." I gave her a big, warm smile and ran my hand through my hair. It'd been a long time since those memories had affected me. A long time since I'd remembered what it was like to be a loser. "Susie."

"Yeah?"

"Are you going to drop them panties for me anytime soon?" I chuckled as she glared at me. She started huffing and puffing and mumbling something under her breath, and I breathed a sigh of relief.

I knew she was pissed off, and I knew she was probably doubting that I was a good man or a good person, but I didn't care. I just needed to ensure she didn't ask me any more questions. I just needed to ensure she didn't try to get anything else out of me.

I just wasn't ready to visit the past again.

FIVE
SUSIE

"There you guys are." Marcia looked up from her spot on the rug as Brody and I made our way back into the campsite.

"Yeah, we won. We went on a walk," I said gruffly, not looking back at Brody. We hadn't spoken for the last forty-five minutes. I couldn't believe he'd asked me when I was going to drop my panties. That wasn't polite or funny.

"You must be really tired," Marcia said.

"Not really. Maybe a little hungry. I could go for another snack."

"It's a good thing we're not hiking Half Dome tomorrow," Finn said. "You guys would be absolutely exhausted."

"I don't even know if I want to do Half Dome," I said. "I don't think I'm physically prepared."

"Don't give up so easily, Susie," Brody interjected. "I'm sure you can do it."

"Yeah. You think me and my panties can do it?" I glared at him, and he just smiled.

"Um, what was that about?" Marcia asked. She wrinkled her brows and tucked a stray hair behind her ears. "Did you just say you and your panties?"

"Why don't you ask him?" I nodded toward Brody. "He's the one that—"

"Okay, Susie. Do we have to get into every single joke I say to you?"

"I don't really think it's a joke when you ask me when I'm going to be dropping my panties."

Marcia gasped, and Finn burst into laughter.

"It's not funny, honey," Marcia chided him.

"I know," Finn said ruefully. He stared at Brody and shook his head. "Dude, really?"

"What?" Brody replied. "I was joking. It's not like I really meant it."

I turned to him. "If I was like, 'Oh, I'd like to drop my panties right now,' you would've said, 'Oh, I was just joking'?"

"Well, of course not." He grinned. "Do I look like a fool?"

"Yeah, you do, actually," I said, and I walked over and sat down on the blanket that had been laid on the ground. It wasn't particularly comfortable, but I didn't want to sit in one of the cramped camping chairs. I leaned back, closed my eyes, and took a couple of deep breaths. "I'm going to kill him if he doesn't get some manners. I'm telling all of you right now so I have several witnesses, and you all know I was driven to it if it happens."

"Um, maybe you shouldn't tell them ahead of time?" Brody said with a cough. "You're not in Florida now."

"What does that mean?" I said, opening my eyes and looking up. He was standing right next to me, looking down at me with a huge grin on his face.

"It just means that you're in California, and premeditated murder doesn't go down so well here."

"You know what, Brody?"

"Yes, Susie?"

"Nothing." I sat up. "So are we going to make s'mores or what?" I looked to Marcia and she nodded.

"I'm down for s'mores and hot chocolate."

"How about spiced hot chocolate?" Finn said as he held up a small flask.

"What's in there?" I asked him suspiciously.

"Only something that will make the hot chocolate taste really good."

"Something like what?"

"Whiskey," he said with a laugh.

"No, thank you. I would rather my hot chocolate just be hot chocolate."

"Ah, you're no fun, Susie," Brody said.

"She's plenty of fun," Marcia said. "Trust me. You don't know the Susie I know."

"I'd like to though," he said, a twinkle in his eyes. I stared at him for a few seconds and kept my mouth shut. I didn't know what was with this guy. Why did he keep teasing me when it was so obvious I wasn't interested in any of his innuendos or games?

"I'm feeling a little bit dirty," I said. "I might go have a quick shower and then come back."

"I'll join you." Marcia jumped up. "You guys get the s'mores and stuff ready. We'll be gone maybe ten, fifteen minutes?"

"You do know it's not a hotel, right?" Brody said. "There's not going to be any sort of luxurious—"

"I do know," I cut him off. "Thank you very much for

reminding me." I turned and looked at Marcia. "And you owe me a trip to a five-star hotel sometime soon."

"Yes, dear," she said. "Let me just work a couple more hours, and maybe I'll save up the money."

"Yeah"—I laughed—"maybe. Come on." We walked toward the showers, and I let out a deep sigh. "Oh my gosh, Marcia, I'm not even joking. That guy is such a jerk."

"I know, I know," she said. "But remember, guys like him are always hiding something by acting that way."

"What do you mean? What the hell is he hiding?"

"He probably has some sort of insecurity or something. I mean, any guy that's that outlandish and that much of a player is overcompensating for something."

"He's probably compensating for a small dick."

"Really, Susie?"

"What? I'm just saying."

"Did you look?"

"What do you mean, did I look? He was wearing jeans."

"So if he wasn't wearing jeans, would you look?"

"Oh my gosh, you're horrible."

"What? I'm just being honest. He is a looker—you've got to admit that."

"I don't have to admit anything, thank you very much."

"So you don't think he's handsome?"

"Well, in a very obvious sort of way. Like that typical, *I'm a baseball player, and I've got a hot body, and*—p"

"Ah, you said hot body."

"Why does this conversation sound very familiar, Marcia?"

"What do you mean?"

"It sounds like a conversation you and I had not so long ago in regards to Finn, and look at me and Finn now."

"Ugh. Well, that's definitely not going to be the

outcome for me and Brody. Literally, as soon as we land at the airport, I'm going home, and I hope to never see him again."

"That might be hard, Susie. He's one of Finn's best friends, and you are my best friend. It's very likely that you'll see each other plenty of times again."

"Oh, Marcia, if I didn't love you..."

"I know, I know. You'd kill me too, right?"

"Yeah. You've got that right." We made our way toward the showers, and I groaned at how gritty and dirty everything was. Brody hadn't been lying. This certainly wasn't the Ritz. Shit, it wasn't even La Quinta Inn.

SIX
BRODY

"Dude, you need to chill." Finn was in my face as soon as the two women left the campsite.

"What?" I blinked at him and held my hands up. "What have I done now?"

"You told her to drop her panties?" He glared at me. "Really?"

"What? I was just testing the waters." I shrugged. "If we're going to get it on in the tent, it will be a lot easier if she has no panties on."

"Susie isn't that sort of girl. Also, she's Marcia's best friend, dude. She's not going anywhere. Don't put me in an awkward position."

"What awkward position?"

"If Marcia doesn't like you, then what do I do?"

"Why wouldn't she like me?" I gave him my megawatt smile. "I'm Brody Wainwright."

"These girls don't care. You're just a guy to them. And right now, you're acting like a douche."

"How was I to know she was going to be so sensitive?"

"These aren't fuckgirls, Brody. Save it for the strip club."

"Why'd you drag me out here then, bro?" I huffed. I could have spent the weekend fucking some bimbo who wouldn't get upset that I flirted with her. "I don't need this shit."

"Maybe I wanted you to get to know my girlfriend." He gave me a pointed look. "Maybe it was important to me for my best friend and my girlfriend to get along."

"Fine." I stared at him for a few seconds. "I'll be on my best behavior."

"Do you have a best behavior?"

"As good as yours was before you met Marcia."

"Yeah, well, she doesn't have to know I was a dog as well. Those days are behind me."

"You're not going to miss it, though?"

"What?"

"The chase. New tail. The thrill of getting her to drop her panties and bra. The feel of sliding into a new pussy. The way they want you. It's all an adrenaline rush."

"It gets old, Brody. It's not the same as looking into the eyes of the woman you love and watching her climax and feeling her love."

"Oh, shit. Did someone get a job working for Hallmark?" I pretended to throw up.

"I can't wait until I see you fall." He gave me an assessing look. "I have a feeling when you fall, it's going to be hard."

"Why do you say that?"

"Because the higher they are, the harder they fall." He grinned. "Love is going to hit you like a ton of bricks. But I promise when it happens, it will be worth it."

"Did Marcia just enter your body?" I narrowed my eyes

and stared at him. "I know these words are not coming out of your mouth."

"Brody Wainwright, if my girl wasn't on this trip with us, I would smack you around."

"You don't have to stop on my account." Marcia laughed as she joined us. Her hair was wet, and her eyes were shining. I found myself looking behind her to see if Susie was there as well. She glanced at me, her hair soaked, long and curly. Her face was free of makeup, and she looked young and earnest. My heart twisted slightly as I took in her appearance of gray sweats and an oversized sweater.

"That was fast," I said, hoping Susie couldn't tell just how excited I was to see her.

"The showers weren't exactly luxurious." Susie wrinkled her nose.

"Understatement of the year." Marcia sidled up next to Finn and put her arm around his waist. He then wrapped his arm around her shoulders and kissed her on the top of the head. They were a vision of domesticity.

"Sickening, eh?" Susie stood next to me and nodded toward Finn and Marcia.

"The lovebirds need to get a room." I licked my lips nervously. "Hey, I just wanted to apologize for earlier. I shouldn't have asked you to drop your panties and bra."

"I don't remember you asking me to remove my bra." Her lips twitched as she stared me in the eyes. "But you're forgiven."

I raised an eyebrow. "Just like that?"

"Yeah." She nodded. "Just like that. I mean, don't do it again."

"Thirty minutes ago, you wanted to bite my head off, and now you're acting like Mother Theresa. What happened in those showers?"

"Trust me, I'm not Mother Theresa." She poked me in the arm. "And just know that if you make a creepy comment like that to me again, I will chop off your dick."

"Ouch." I rubbed the front of my jeans instinctively. "That would hurt."

"Very much." She nodded.

"So I won't be making a comment like that again—even if you beg me."

"Even if I beg you?" She threw her head back and started laughing. Sprinkles of water flew off her curls and hit my skin. "I wouldn't worry about that."

"Hey, you're getting me wet." I showed her my arm, and she rolled her eyes.

"You wish, Brody."

"I wish?" I frowned, and then my eyes widened as she gave me a wicked look. "Wait, what? Did you just make a dirty joke?"

"I don't know, did I?" She gave me a sexy wink, and something in my pants expanded. Shit, that was unexpected. Susie had a sense of humor I hadn't seen coming.

"Don't get used to them. Okay, so what's next?"

"S'mores, I guess." I shrugged. "And horror stories."

"Oh, I hate scary stories." She shivered.

"But you love telling them." Marcia split away from Finn and joined us again. "Susie is a story queen."

"I wouldn't say queen. Maybe a princess."

"Now I'm curious." I stared at her lips as she laughed. "Please do tell us a story."

"I wouldn't want to give you an excuse to jump into my sleeping bag..."

"I don't need an excuse." I grinned. "You say the word and I'm there."

"Are you two flirting?" Marcia sounded excited, and

Susie shook her head vehemently. A shimmer of disappointment filled me as she pretended to retch.

"No way. We just decided to be buddies seeing as we have a super long hike coming up, and we're probably going to be doing it together while you and Finn canoodle."

"We do not canoodle." Marcia giggled girlishly. "Okay, maybe a little, but he's just so damn sweet and hot."

"Is someone talking about me?" Finn headed over to us with two steaming mugs of hot chocolate in his hands. "Here you go, girls. Hot chocolate with no good stuff."

"Thanks, Finn." Susie smiled at him warmly, and I knew that I wanted her to look at me like that. The only looks she gave me were disgusted and/or annoyed--similar to the girls in high school. But I knew she was different.

"Where's my cup?"

"You want hot chocolate, or you want whiskey?"

"Whiskey all day, every day." I lifted up my hand for a high five. "Shall we sit around the fire?"

"Let's do it." Finn grabbed Marcia by the hand and spun her around as they headed toward the fire. Susie stared at me as we made our way as well, and we shared a look that said we were both exasperated and delighted for our friends.

SEVEN
SUSIE

The fire was warm and kept me toasty as I sat in the gray camping chair. The flames leapt back and forth, illuminating Brody's face as he messily ate s'mores. I felt content and happy, which surprised me seeing as I'd wanted to kill Brody only a few hours before. Though, I supposed we were both taking a truce. I couldn't stop myself from studying Brody's face as he sat there, more relaxed than I'd ever seen him. He didn't have his guard up or his macho façade going, and there was a vulnerability to him that I was surprised to see.

Jocks weren't vulnerable. They didn't have soft sides.

But maybe I'd been wrong.

"Okay, Susie. It's your turn to tell us a story." Marcia prodded me from her position on Finn's lap. He had his arms wrapped around her as he nuzzled the side of her neck, and all of a sudden, I felt emotional.

I was jealous. Not that I wasn't deliriously happy for Marcia, but I wanted that for myself as well. I wanted to fall in love. I wanted someone to look at me the way Finn looked at Marcia. I wanted to feel butterflies in my stomach.

I wanted to experience the first kiss that made my heart leap for joy. I wanted to touch someone who smiled at me with love in their eyes. I wanted to *be* in love.

Not only did I want to be in love but I wanted it to be with someone that was head over heels for me. I wanted what Marcia had. I was so happy that she had met the love of her life, but it felt like everything good was happening to her, and nothing good was happening to me. She found a job, she had new friends, and now she had love.

And what did I have?

"Are you gonna tell us that story, or what?" Brody looked at me, and I wondered what it would be like to kiss him.

"Okay, but I don't want you to get scared. Once upon a time, there were four people..."

"Once upon a time?" Brody asked. "Is this a fairy tale? Is it going to end with The Wicked Witch of the West doing something?"

"Are you going to let me finish?" I replied. "Or would you rather tell a story instead?"

"Don't get your knickers in a twist." He paused and wiggled his tongue at me. "And when I say don't get your knickers in a twist, I don't mean drop them for me."

"Really?" Finn stared at his friend. "The night was going so well."

"It still is," I said with a smile. "Now, Brody, shut up so I can actually tell my story."

"I love it when you talk dirty to me."

We both started laughing. He was incorrigible, but there was something about his personality I was starting to like. He wasn't a jackass like I had originally thought. He definitely was arrogant, but there was a caring side to him as well.

"I'm going to continue," I said.

"But..."

"But what, Brody?"

"Just as long as it's not a fairy tale. I don't want to hear about Cinderella or Snow White or Sleeping Beauty or—"

"Sounds like you know a lot of different Disney princesses. I guess we know what you do on the weekends." I started laughing, and Marcia grinned at me.

"Very funny." Brody shook his head. "But I'll be quiet now."

"Thank you. Now, is everyone settled in? Can I continue?"

"You may continue, Susie," Finn said wryly, and then he looked to Marcia. "Is she always a bossy boots like this?"

"Yep." She grinned.

"Hey, that's not fair. I'm not a bossy boots."

"You just take charge," Marcia continues, "and I'm very thankful for it. If you didn't have that kind of personality, then we would've been kicked out of our apartment a very long time ago."

"You can say that again," I said with a smile. "Okay. So once upon a time, there were four people."

"Ooh." Brody made howling noises.

"And they were at Yosemite," I said.

"They were at Yosemite just like us?" Brody raised an eyebrow.

"Brody, enough." I glared at him.

"Sorry, sorry. I will be quiet." He pretended to zip his lips and I grinned.

"And they were at Yosemite. It was a dark, spooky night, and there was barely a star to see in the sky," I said in lowered tones. "The moon was bright, and they could hear the howling of wolves."

"Wolves? Like werewolves?" Marcia spoke up, and I shushed her. "Sorry, Susie."

"It's okay. But they could hear the howling of wolves. They weren't sure if it was werewolves or not. So, two of the men decided to go check."

"Why does it always have to be the men?" Finn said. Before I could say anything, he rushed out, "Sorry. My bad."

"Uh-huh. And the two men," I continued, "decided to go check out where the howls were coming from." I looked around the campsite. The fire was jumping, and I could hear an owl hooting in the distance. I grinned. "One of the women at the campsite decided that she was going to go check on the men, but the other woman didn't want to go."

"Why don't they stay together?" Marcia said. "Who's dumb enough to venture out on their own in this day and age?"

"Marcia." I glared at her. "You guys are killing the vibe. You can't interrupt me as I'm telling my story. Would you interrupt Hans Christian Andersen, or The Brothers Grimm or Walt Disney?"

"I don't know," Brody said dryly. "Are you telling us that you're the reincarnation of one of them?"

"Obviously not."

"Guys," Finn said. "I, for one, want to hear the end of the story."

"Me too," Marcia said eagerly. "Susie tells the best stories."

"I'm listening," Brody said. "Continue, please."

"If someone interrupts me again, I'm not going to." I paused as a rustle came from the trees behind me. I froze and looked at everyone. "What was that?"

"What was what?" Brody said, shaking his head.

"I heard something in the leaves."

He shrugged. "It's most probably a bear."

"I thought you were joking."

"Why would I joke about bears?"

"It's fine," Finn said. "The bears won't bother us here. It's more likely a lizard, or maybe a skunk or raccoon looking for food. That's why I told everyone to pack up everything tightly so we don't get visitors of the scavenger kind."

"Okay," I said. "Well, anyway. One of the girls went off into the woods by herself, looking for the men. She saw a figure in the distance standing, next to one of the trees."

"What sort of tree?" Brody said and then zipped his lips again.

"She saw a figure in the distance," I repeated, "and she walked up to it thinking it was one of the men. And then, the figure turned toward her, and she gasped."

"What was it?" Marcia said, and I smiled sinisterly.

"The figure started to howl and bared its teeth in the moonlight. It was the wolf they'd all been hearing previously. And the wolf said, 'You've come, beautiful princess.'"

"I thought this wasn't a fairy tale," Brody said.

"Brody," I shouted. "I'm not finishing the story."

"I'm sorry, I'm sorry. Please finish the story. I want to know what happens."

"Really?" I folded my arms. "I feel like you're just making fun of me now."

"I promise I'm not. I want to know what happened with the princess and the werewolf." His lips twitched. "And who knows, maybe there's going to be a baseball player thrown in there somewhere as well."

"You know what, Brody Wainwright?"

"Yes, Susie?"

"You're just incorrigible."

"I've heard that one before."

"Guys, if you're going to flirt, can you do it after the story?" Finn said with a grin, and Marcia hit him in the shoulder.

"Finn," she chastised.

"What?" he said. "I'm just calling it like it is."

"We're not flirting," I said.

"I just want to know what happens with this werewolf and this princess," Brody said.

"I swear," I said, "if anyone interrupts me again..."

"Yeah, yeah. You're not going to tell us the rest of the story," Brody said.

"Anyway. The werewolf started whistling, and the princess got confused because she didn't know werewolves could whistle." I stared at Brody, and I could tell he wanted to interrupt. His lips were twitching, and he was running his hands through his hair as he sat forward, but he didn't say anything.

Marcia's eyes were focused on me in rapt attention, and Finn had put his phone back into his pants pocket. I loved making up stories, especially to audiences that were engaged and would listen.

"So she walked over to the werewolf and she said—"

"Excuse me," a loud voice sounded from behind us.

"Ahh!" I jumped up and ran toward the tent.

"Oh, sorry." A tall guy stepped in. "I'm Ken. I'm your camp neighbor." He gave us a bemused grin. "I didn't mean to scare you."

"No worries," I said, stepping back from the tent. Brody was laughing now, and so was Finn. Marcia jumped up and walked over to me.

"You okay, Susie?"

"Yeah, I just wasn't expecting someone else to talk just then."

"You got caught up in your own story, huh?" Brody said with a laugh.

"I guess I did."

"Can we help you?" Brody said to the guy.

"I was actually just wondering if you had any water. I should have brought much more than I did, but I drank the bottle that I had and, well, I'm thirsty."

"Sure," Finn said. "Let me get you some." The two men walked over to Finn's truck.

Marcia was smiling at me. "You're not going to tell us for the rest of the story tonight, are you?"

"Nope. I was interrupted far too many times."

"Well, that disappoints me," Brody said, and he smiled warmly. "I was hoping to hear what happened with the wolf and the princess."

"Really, Brody?"

"You're a good storyteller. Have you ever thought about being an actress?"

"Not really. At one point in my life, I kind of did. But no."

"What about a writer?"

"That would be cool, but I don't know that it's my passion."

"She'd be great. She'd be really, really great," Marcia said, speaking up. "I'd like to shoot and direct movies, and I'd love for Susie to write the scripts. We'd be a dynamic duo."

"You're already a dynamic duo," Brody said. He looked at his watch and yawned. "I guess I should go brush my teeth and get ready for bed."

"Oh, what time is it?" I said in surprise. I looked at my

own watch and gasped. "Oh my gosh. It's close to midnight."

He nodded. "It got late, huh? It's a good thing we're not hiking Half Dome tomorrow."

"Yeah," I said. "Though I don't know that I'm going to be able to do it the day after either."

"Positive mental attitude, Susie. You can do anything you put your mind to."

"Um, I don't think that's true," I said dryly. "If I put my mind to climbing Mount Everest, could I do it?"

"Yeah," he said. "With lots of training."

"Exactly. With lots of training, which I don't have. I also don't have training for Half Dome."

"It'll be okay," he said softly. "And if at any point you want to stop and turn around, I'll stop with you."

"You don't have to do that."

"I know I don't have to, but I'd be more than happy to. I just came along for the ride. This is Finn's dream. And if you feel like you can't go any further, I'll turn back with you. Promise."

I looked at him with suspicious eyes, and then I realized that he was being sincere and sweet, and it surprised me.

"Thank you," I said.

"Wow, that sounded almost genuine."

"It was genuine," I said.

"Well, then I think we're making headway, Susie."

"I think we are as well, Brody. Now you should go brush your teeth because I don't want you stinking up the tent with bad breath."

"And she's back," he said with a laugh. I grinned at him as he made his way to the campsite. Marcia gave me a look, and I frowned.

"What's that expression on your face about?"

"You two seem to be getting awfully cozy and friendly."

"I wouldn't say that. I think we're barely stabbing each other because we're stuck on this trip together."

"Me thinks you protest too much." She smiled. "I'm glad you're getting along. It's important that you like Finn's best friend. It just makes life easier."

"I know," I said softly. "Don't worry. I won't mess this up. I know how important it is for me to get along with Finn's friends."

"I love you. You know that, Susie?"

"Love you, Marcia."

EIGHT

BRODY

I brushed my teeth back and forth quickly, anxious to get back to the campsite and spend more time talking to Susie. She was fun and funny and engaging, and there was a light to her that I'd never seen in another human being. She had a way with words that drew me in and made me want to listen to her beautiful, melodic voice. I wanted to tease her just to see the sparkle in her eyes.

I wanted to get back to continue my conversation with her, tease her some more, and just be around her, which was a strange feeling to me. I'd never wanted to be around anyone before. Everyone in my life had always been disposable—other than Finn. Everyone had their purpose and meaning, and it was weird, because she didn't really fit into any of those boxes.

She wasn't a teammate I had to discuss the job with. She wasn't one of my attorneys or managers I had to discuss money with. She wasn't one of my guy friends I talked to about chicks and cars. And she wasn't a family member I had idle chatter with. She was Susie, and she was funny and vibrant, and I could talk about anything with her. At least, that's how I felt.

I walked back to the campsite, clutching my toothbrush and grinning. There were two guys walking ahead of me, and one of them started singing the old Kenny Rogers song, "Gambler." But as I listened carefully, I realized they had changed the lyrics.

"You got to know when to fuck 'em," one guy said.

"You got to know when to slap them," the other one said, and they both started laughing. The first guy started singing again, but this time, he sang the correct lyrics.

And suddenly, I stopped. That song had been an old family favorite of mine and my brothers. Memories came crashing through.

We'd been on our grandparents' farm in Kentucky and sitting on bales of hay. My eldest brother had stolen a pack of cigarettes, and we lit one up and smoked, coughing and huffing and puffing—hating the taste of tobacco but wanting to feel like men.

I'd been talking about the periodic table and different elements, and my brother's eyes had been glazed over, bored, and I'd laid back and wished I was anywhere but there. I'd wished I had brothers that understood me.

I'd wished I had brothers that cared about things other than sports.

But in those days, when I'd felt like I wasn't being listened to or I'd felt like I didn't belong, I'd sing a country music song like Kenny Rogers or Dolly Parton, and we'd all chorus together. I wasn't sure why music had been the thing that made us gel, but it was. Any uncomfortable moment, any time when one of us felt upset or mad, we'd sing.

"Gambling Man," I mumbled under my breath, staring

into the night sky. I hadn't spoken to anyone in my family for a long time. In fact, I tried not to think about them too much. They were beyond proud of me now that I was a baseball player and played for the Yankees—now that I was someone they understood. But there was always the undercurrent of anger and bitterness and hurt, and the untold sadness that none of us shared throughout my family. They always made me feel tense.

"Hey, sleepyhead."

I blinked and looked up, and there was Susie, standing right in front of me. Her worried eyes darted back and forth as she smiled sweetly, and in that moment, she looked like an angel. Her fingers reached up and played with one of her curls as she shifted her weight to the side. She chewed on her lower lip, and for a few moments, we just stood there in silence, sizing each other up.

"Hey, what's up?" I asked her. "Were you looking for me?"

"No, I was coming to brush my teeth, and I saw you just standing there. Did you get lost?" she asked jokingly, but we both knew that wasn't possible in a campsite as small as this.

I shrugged. "I was just thinking and looking at the stars. Seeing if I could name any of the constellations."

"Oh." She nodded, and something passed in her eyes that told me she knew it was a lie.

"So, I'm going to go brush my teeth, and then I guess we'll head to the tent?" She made a face. Finn and Marcia have already gone to bed."

"I don't think they've gone to bed." I winked at her, and she groaned.

"You know what I mean."

"I do," I said with a smile. "You want me to walk with you back to the bathroom and then walk back?"

"Oh, no. You don't have to do that."

"I know I don't, but I don't want the big, bad wolf to get you."

"I think you might be the big, bad wolf, Brody Wainwright." She grinned at me, and I could see that she was staring at my lips, and all I could do was stare at hers. All I could think about was what her lips would taste like. What she would feel like pressed against my body. If she would scream and cry out when I made her come. If she would dig her fingernails into my back, begging me to take her.

"Hey, you okay?" she said again, and I blinked.

"Yeah, I'm fine." I shifted slightly. I was hard. She stared at me, blushing.

"So, I'm going to go brush my teeth now, and you do not have to come with me, but I'll see you in the tent?" she said and gave me a timid smile.

"Yeah, I'll be there," I said and nodded. I made sure she made her way to the bathroom before I walked back to our campsite. The fire was out, and Finn and Marcia were giggling from inside their tent.

"Night, guys. Don't do anything I wouldn't do," I said loudly, and I heard Finn grunt.

"Night, night, Brody," he responded. "Be a good boy."

"I'm always a good boy," I said and laughed as I unzipped the tent. I looked inside and saw the two sleeping bags lying next to each other. I wasn't sure which one Susie wanted, so I decided to wait before I got into it. I sat on top of one of the bags and thought for a couple of seconds.

I was surprised that my mood wasn't more melancholy after thinking about my family. I'd gone to a bad place for a couple of minutes, but as soon as I'd seen Susie and her worried expression and nervous smile, all I could think about was her.

I wondered what my life would've been like if I'd had a

friend like her in high school. Someone I could count on and that would be a good listener and be there to take my mind off everything else. I wondered what my life would look like today if I'd pursued my real passion and gone into the sciences. Where would I be if I'd tried to become a chemist?

I knew there was no point in thinking about the past. I was a baseball player—one of the MVPs of the previous season. I was a somebody. I was a jock. I chuckled to myself as I thought about it.

Me, Brody Wainwright, a jock.

When I was a teenager, I never would've believed it. But here I was, doing all the things that jocks did just to prove myself to my family, and to the world, that I was someone. That I mattered. That everything that had happened in the past hadn't been in vain.

There was a rustling outside the tent, and I sat up, grinning as Susie made her way inside.

"You're still up?" She looked surprised as she stepped inside.

"You really thought I was going to fall asleep within five minutes?"

"I don't know. A lot of guys can fall asleep pretty fast."

"Well, not me. I wasn't sure which tent you wanted."

"Which tent?" she said.

"I meant which sleeping bag." I grinned. "Sorry. My mind's all over the place."

"That's okay." She smiled. "You're sitting on one sleeping bag, so I think I'll take the other one."

"Oh, I didn't even think about that."

"No worries. They're both the same, right?"

"Yeah." She unzipped her sleeping bag and slipped

inside, and then I jumped up and unzipped mine and slipped inside as well.

"I'm going to turn out the flashlight. Is that okay?" I pointed toward the light that was hanging from the top of the tent.

"Sure," she said. I pressed the power button and turned it off, and we were enveloped in darkness. We lay there in silence. All I could hear were the sounds of Finn and Marcia giggling from the tent next to us and birds in the distance. Then there was a rustling in the trees, and she gasped.

"It's okay, Susie," I said. "Nothing will harm you with me here."

"Um, you're going to protect me from the bears?" There was a nervous tone in her voice.

"Yeah. If a bear comes in here, I'll offer myself up first. Promise."

"You don't have to do that, but thank you."

"I know I don't have to, but I'm a man. I'll protect you."

"Oh, boy. You're a macho man."

"Is there something wrong with that?"

"No, I guess not."

"You seem like you're scared, and I'm not scared, so I'll step in front of a bear for you."

She giggled. "Why does that sound like a marriage vow?"

"A marriage vow?" I shuddered. "What does that mean?"

"I don't know," she said. "It just sounds like someone would say it when they're at the altar. "I take you to be my lawfully wedded wife, and if a bear happens upon us, I'll stand in front of it for you," she said in a loud, deep voice, and I chuckled.

"You're goofy, you know that?"

"I know," she said. "That's how I like it."

"It must be nice having a best friend like Marcia. Someone you've known your whole life. I guess the two of you really complement each other?"

"Yeah," she said. "I guess I'm the dependable stalwart in the friendship."

"Oh? What does that mean?"

"Nothing," she said quickly. "And you and Finn— you've been friends for a long time too?"

"Yeah, since college. He's a good guy."

"I know," she said. "He's treated Marcia really well, and I'm glad they've found each other."

"Are you seeing anyone?"

"No. Just haven't met the one yet."

"But you're looking?"

"Aren't we all looking?" she said softly.

"No." I shook my head, though I realized she couldn't see me. "I'm not looking.

"Wow. Why doesn't that surprise me?"

"I don't know. Why doesn't it?"

"You don't seem like the sort of guy that's interested in settling down."

And as she said the words, I realized how true they were, but I also realized how much I wanted to change them.

NINE

SUSIE

The leaves in the trees rustled outside of the tent, and an owl hooted in the distance. I blinked in the dark, trying to adjust my eyesight, and scratched my head as a mosquito flew by me.

"Oh, man," I mumbled under my breath as I swat at it.

"What is it?" Brody asked me, concern in his voice.

"Nothing. I think I let a mosquito into the tent when I was coming in."

"Oh no, that sucks. I have some mosquito repellent if you want to put it on."

"No, that's okay. Thank you, though."

"Are you sure?"

"Yeah. I mean, I would, but I know how much it smells, and I don't want to keep the both of us up."

"It's okay. I wouldn't have offered it if I couldn't deal," he said. "Are you sure you don't want to put it on?"

"No, thanks. That was really sweet of you."

"I'm a sweet guy," he said in his deep, husky voice. I felt him roll over so that he was facing me, and I rolled over so that I was facing him. I could just about make out his face in the darkness.

"I'm falling asleep," I said, yawning as he stared at me.

"I'm falling asleep too."

"Then I guess I should say good night."

"Good night, Susie." There was mirth in his voice, and I couldn't stop myself from laughing. "What's so funny?" he asked, moving closer to me.

"You are. I hate to say it, because you're already full of yourself, but you're funny."

"Funny as in ha-ha, or funny as in I look weird?"

"You know you don't look weird, Brody."

"I don't know. My good looks and charm haven't worked on you thus far."

"Your good looks and charm will never work on me, but that doesn't mean I can't tell you that I think you're good looking."

"So you do think I'm good looking, then?"

"You know you are."

"Perhaps," he said with shrug. "But maybe I'm someone that didn't grow up with good looks."

There was a hint of seriousness in his voice that led me to believe he was speaking the truth. I was thoughtful for a few seconds, unsure of how to respond to his comments. There were moments when I actually thought there was a depth to Brody Wainwright that I never would've believed.

He wasn't meaningful all of the time, but in those rare moments, I felt something real from him.

"Oh?" I said lightly. "You weren't always a looker?"

"Believe it or not, I wasn't," he said softly.

"I find it hard to believe."

"I didn't blossom until college when I joined the baseball team. I was a walk-on with Finn. I'm not sure if I told you that already."

"Oh, yeah. I think you may have mentioned it. So you didn't play in high school, then?"

"Nope. I was a nerd, remember?"

"I just can't wrap my head around you being a nerd."

"Well, listen to this."

"What?"

He cleared his throat. "Hi-ho, little Bobby Brown caught napping—"

"What?" I interrupted him. "What are you saying?"

"It's the periodic table. It's how I remembered it."

"What do you mean?"

"Hi, hydrogen. Ho, helium. Little, lithium. Brown—tell me if you can guess what that is."

I laughed. "I have absolutely no idea."

"Come on. Guess, Susie."

"What did you say it began with again?"

"B. Be."

"Um, I don't know. Bear?"

"No, silly. Periodic table."

"I don't know. Tell me."

"Beryllium."

"Um, never heard of it before in my life."

"You never took chemistry?" He sounded surprised.

"I did, but I guess I wasn't that good at it. So, wow. You really remember it based on that rhyme?"

"Yeah. Hi-ho, little Bobby Brown caught napping on Friday night. Naughty Maggie always sings pop songs."

"Wow," I said again. "So, that's a periodic table."

"Yeah, those are the elements."

"You can still remember what they stand for?"

"Yep," he said. "Hydrogen, helium, lithium, beryllium,

boron, carbon, nitrogen, oxygen." He cleared his throat. "Fluorine, neon, sodium—because NA is sodium."

"Okay, if you say so."

"Magnesium, aluminum, silicone, phosphorus, sulfur."

"Wow. That's really cool."

"Chlorine, argon, potassium—and potassium is K."

"Are you going to recite the entire periodic table?"

"No." He started laughing. "Fun first date I am, huh?" He stopped himself. "Well, not technically a first date, but our first night together. And not even technically our first night together. Well, not in that sense anyway."

"Yeah, not in that sense at all," I said.

"So do you enjoy camping?"

"You're just changing the subject?" I said, surprised. "I thought you were telling me all about chemistry."

"Didn't we already establish that I don't want to bore you?"

"It doesn't bore me if it excites you. I'm just surprised. I've never met a jock that's into chemistry before."

"Have you met many jocks?"

"No, not really. I wasn't in that crowd in high school, and definitely not in college."

"I wasn't in that crowd in high school either," he said softly. "In fact, I hated jocks when I was in high school."

"Really?" It was my turn to be surprised. How was it that Brody Wainwright, star baseball player, had hated jocks when he was in high school? That didn't make sense. He was a jock, maybe the biggest jock of them all. I knew there was a story there, but I didn't want to be nosy and pry.

"So, you like camping?" he asked.

"Not really. It's not Marcia's and my thing, to be honest."

"What do you and Marcia like to do?"

"Shop, go to lunch, read, watch movies, go to the theater, play board games, go hiking—actually, that's a lie."

"You don't like hiking?" he said.

"Well, we like going for walks, which is very different from hiking. We'll walk around the mall. But when most people hear hiking, they think something different."

He chuckled. "Like climbing Half Dome."

"Oh my gosh. Don't remind me. I don't know how I'm going to make this climb."

"You'll be fine, Susie."

"We'll see," I said. "Do you like camping?"

"I haven't been camping in a while," he said. "When I was younger, my brothers and I used to go camping a lot. My grandparents were kind of country, you know? So we learned to shoot and hunt and fish. So, yeah, I was into it back then."

"Do you and your brothers go camping a lot now?"

"No," he said abruptly. "Can I ask you something?"

"Yeah." I wondered why he changed the subject. I could tell by the harsh tone in his voice that he didn't want to talk about his family.

What had happened? Were his brothers jealous of his success? Had one of his brothers slept with his girlfriend? There was a story there, and I wanted to get to the bottom of it, but I wasn't going to ask.

"Have you ever kissed in the dark?"

"What?" I started laughing. His question was so out of left field.

"That wasn't the response I was expecting," he said huskily. "Can I tell you something?"

I could feel his face getting closer to mine. My body was warming, and I was slightly out of breath, even though he wasn't even touching me.

"What are you going to tell me? More chemistry?"

"Well, did you know the nucleus—" He stopped and started laughing. "No, that's not what I wanted to tell you. And actually, I changed my mind. I'm not going to tell you now."

"You can't do that," I said softly.

"I can't do what?"

"You can't tell me you're going to tell me something and then not tell me. That's not fair."

"I changed my mind."

"But now I'm always going to be wondering what you were going to tell me."

"I don't think you'd care that much."

"I do. I want to know."

"I don't want to get into trouble."

"What do you mean? How are you going to get in trouble?"

"Because if I tell you what I wanted to tell you, then you're going to be upset, and you're going to tell Marcia, who's going to tell Finn, who's going to blow up at me and say that I'm ruining his relationship."

"I promise I won't say anything."

"Well, I don't know that I want to risk it."

"Oh my gosh, Brody. What were you going to tell me?"

"I was just going to tell you that the first time I saw you, I thought you were very pretty."

"Well, thank you."

"And I thought you had beautiful lips."

"Okay." I could feel my face warming as I smiled. I was grateful we were in the dark, and he couldn't see how happy he was making me.

"And I was also going to tell you that I thought you had a wicked..."

"What? You thought I had a wicked what?"

"I better stop while I'm ahead."

"Tell me."

"I'm not going to tell you."

"Brody, tell me."

"Why? So you can tell me off?"

"I'm not going to tell you off."

He unzipped his sleeping bag.

"What are you doing?" I asked.

"I'm feeling warm, so I'm going to lie on top of it for a little bit."

"Oh, okay," I said.

"Are you feeling warm too?"

"A little bit."

"I can help you unzip it if you want," he said, and before I knew what was happening, he was unzipping the bag all the way down. I could feel his breath close to my face as he leaned over me. His eyes were looking into mine, and he was grinning. "So, Susie."

"Yes, Brody?"

"I was thinking..."

"Yeah?"

"That you have a really nice rack."

"Really? How old are you? Who says rack?"

"Would you rather me say breasts or tits or titties or boobies? I thought you had a fine set of boobies."

"But you've never seen my boobies," I said softly. He groaned then and stepped back so that he was on his own sleeping bag.

"You're flirting with me, aren't you?" he asked.

"Me?" I said innocently. "How am I flirting with you? You're the one that brought up my boobies."

"I can tell from your tone that you're trying to tease and seduce me."

"I didn't know I had a tone, Brody."

"Oh, yeah?" he said, and then his arms wound around me, and he was tickling me. I started giggling loudly, as I was very ticklish, and I tried to push him back.

"No, you can't tickle me," I said as I reached my hands up and tried to tickle him too. I was giggling harder and harder, and we started wrestling around on the sleeping bags. "Brody Wainwright, I'm going to get you," I said as he pushed me back.

"Not if I get you first." We were both laughing and rolling around until, suddenly, we both stopped. I was breathing heavily as I straddled him. His hands were pressed under mine, and I grinned down at him.

"I got you exactly where I want you."

"Something tells me you really want me," he said huskily. I realized then that I was sitting on top of him. That I could feel his hardness between my legs. I quickly rolled off and lay on top of my sleeping bag.

"Well, I didn't anticipate having a tickling match tonight," I said.

"Me neither," he said as he reached over and brushed the hair away from my face. "But I'm glad that we did."

"Why is that?"

"Why do you think?" he said.

I swallowed hard. Brody had a way of turning me on with the things he didn't say or do. I was definitely beginning to understand why he had so many women under his spell.

TEN

BRODY

I could still feel Susie's hair tickling the side of my face, even though she was now on top of her own sleeping bag. I looked over at her, and I could tell she was slightly embarrassed, but also slightly turned on, which was an understatement for me. I had a hard-on as tall and stiff as Plymouth Rock, and it didn't seem like it was going to lessen in size anytime soon. Normally, in situations like these, I would roll over and pull her into my arms, kiss her, and touch her softly before eventually making her mine. But this wasn't a normal situation. Susie wasn't someone I could just fuck. She wasn't someone I could just have a night of fun with and forget about in the morning.

For one, I didn't want to do that. And for two, if I did, Finn would absolutely kill me and would probably end our friendship, and I wasn't willing to risk that. He was a good guy, and I quite liked hanging out with him, Marcia, and Susie.

"You surprise me," Susie said softly, her voice barely a whisper. She had a sexy voice, and I wondered if she knew how much it turned me on when she spoke in the dark. I could listen to her talk all night.

"How so?" I chewed on my lower lip. I wanted to make a comment about her being surprised at how hard my dick had felt against her when she'd been on top of me just now, but I was trying to be a better man. I was trying to be more appropriate, even though it was very hard for me—pun intended.

"I just thought you would've had me on my back by now," she said with a girlish giggle.

"Oh?" I was getting even harder now.

"Yeah." She leaned closer to me, and I could see her peering at me. "I thought you were some sort of playboy. I thought you'd have your wicked way with me."

"I'm trying to be respectful, Susie," I said as I moved closer to her. My hand found the side of her face, and I brushed hairs away from her forehead. Her lips trembled slightly, and I rubbed my thumb against them. "I don't want to do anything you'll regret."

"I wouldn't let you do anything I'd regret," she said, staring at me unabashedly.

"Are you coming on to me, Susie?"

"No." She shook her head quickly. "I was just saying I'm surprised, you know, given your reputation."

"My reputation precedes me, I assume."

"I guess it does."

"But I'm curious. What do you know of my reputation? I thought you weren't interested in sports, and you had absolutely no idea who I was."

"Well, I don't, but—" She looked away quickly.

"What? What is it? I'm curious."

"Google is my friend, and I looked you up."

"Ah, I see. So you know all about me now, do you?"

"Not really. Surprisingly, there wasn't that much information about you other than the baseball teams that you've played on and the many women you've dated."

"Ah, the models and the actresses—even a princess or two."

"You dated a princess?" she said, her eyes widening in shock. I could tell by the way she was staring directly in my eyes that she was trying to figure out if I was telling the truth or not.

"Well, I don't know that she would call it dating. I certainly wouldn't."

"Oh," she said. "Wow."

"Wow indeed." I laughed. "So what do you imagine I would've done if you weren't Finn's girlfriend's best friend?"

"I don't know," she said.

"Perhaps I would've kissed you," I said, moving my lips closer to hers, but not touching them. "And then perhaps I would've run my fingers down your arms like this." I ran them softly down the side of her arms, and she shivered.

"And then perhaps my hand would've slid to your stomach." My hand moved to her stomach and slid her T-shirt up so that the palm of my hand was resting against her skin. It was warm, and I could feel her heart beating through her skin.

"Finn wouldn't like this," she said.

"But does Finn have to know?"

"No. What would you have done next?"

"Then I would've moved my hand up." My fingers inched their way up her stomach and stopped right underneath her right breast.

She gasped. "And then?"

"And then my hand would have cupped you." I ran my fingers across her bra and then pulled them away. "And I would have slipped your breast out of your bra and teased you, squeezing your nipple before bending my head to kiss and suck. Do I need to go on?"

"You're not going to show me?" she said breathlessly.

I could hear the stress and tension in her voice. I could tell she wanted me to touch her as badly as I wanted to. She was as caught up in the moment as I was, and if she were anyone else, if I cared even just a little bit less, I would've made her mine.

I licked my lips slowly and then gazed down at her beautiful face. Because even though it was dark and shadowed, I could still make out the outline. I could still see her eyes, wide and innocent, staring up at me.

"Are you a virgin, Susie?" I asked her softly, my lips mere inches from hers.

"No." She laughed—a loud sound that delighted me. "Why would you think I'm a virgin?"

"I don't know. Perhaps you just act like one."

"How does one act like a virgin?"

I pressed my lips against hers, unable to stop myself. She kissed me back and wrapped her arms around my neck. Her fingers were in my hair, and I moaned against her lips as I slipped my hand up the side of her shirt and cupped her breast. I adjusted myself on top of her so she could feel the full weight of me, and she opened her legs. My tongue entered her mouth, and she sucked on it eagerly, her fingers now on my back, running down so they could slip inside my T-shirt. Her hands traveled my warm skin, and I'd never felt more alive in my life.

I pulled away then and gave her one kiss on the forehead. "Now, now, Susie. I'm going to think you're trying to seduce me."

"Well, Mr. Wainwright," she whispered in my ear, "perhaps I am."

ELEVEN
SUSIE

"So who's ready to hike Half Dome this morning?" Finn's voice sounded unbearably cheerful as I exited the tent.

"Not me." I shook my head. "I'm feeling really nervous, guys. I'm not even trying to downplay this, but I'm not a hiker."

"It'll be okay," Finn said. "Right, Brody?"

"Yeah, it'll be fine, Susie." Brody held up his cup of coffee and smiled at me. There was a warm expression on his face, and I smiled back at him. We hadn't yet talked about our little dalliance a couple of nights earlier, and the previous day had gone fairly smoothly.

We'd done some shorter hikes around Yosemite, and after we'd eaten dinner and cleaned up, I'd fallen asleep. I'd been surprised because my body had been anticipating some more kissing and perhaps some touching, but I'd been exhausted. I'd woken up this morning expecting him to have some sort of joke for me, but he hadn't been in the tent. He must have gotten up a lot earlier than me. They were already sitting here drinking coffee, fully dressed.

"Hey, sleepyhead," Finn said as Marcia exited their tent.

She yawned. "Morning."

I looked over at my best friend and her pretty face. "Morning. I'm just getting up too."

"I'm tired," she said.

"Yeah, well, that's because it's six o'clock in the morning," Finn said.

I groaned. "I wish you hadn't set alarms for that early."

"If we're going to hike Half Dome, we have to start early," Finn said. "I'm not trying to scare you girls, because it's not the craziest climb, but it is intense."

"I don't like the sound of intense." I was starting to get worried. I wasn't in the best shape of my life, and I didn't like the sound of an intense hike.

"It'll be okay."

Brody stood up and walked over to me, a mug in his hand. "This is for you."

"What is it?"

"A special tea."

"A special tea! Not even coffee?"

"No." He shook his head. "This will give you the pep you need without the crash. Trust me."

"Oh, what's in it?"

"It's got some ginger, honey, lemon, and—"

"This sounds like a tea I would drink if I had a cold or a flu or something."

"Trust me. It's also got some turmeric."

"Turmeric?"

"Yeah, you'll see."

I stared at him. "I guess."

"Just try it, Susie. You'll like it."

I took a sip, and surprisingly, it tasted pretty good. "So

this is going to give me energy to run up the mountain, then?"

"I don't know about run, but it will definitely get you moving."

"Okay, if you say so. I'm kind of hungry too."

"Breakfast coming right up, girls," Finn said. "We can't have anything too heavy, so I've made some oatmeal, and then we also have some eggs and toast."

"Sounds good to me." I nodded my agreement, as I wanted to get my mind off the upcoming hike.

"And then I'm going to bring apples and granola bars and lots and lots of water." Brody added, holding up a backpack.

"Okay. Is there anything else we should bring?" I wasn't sure why I asked because. It wasn't like I'd brought anything in preparation for the hike, other than my hiking boots.

"I've made sandwiches," Finn said. "For when we stop for lunch."

"It sounds like you guys have it all sorted." I shrugged and tried to ignore the nerves in my stomach. I really wished I was about to go lie on a beach as opposed to climb a mountain. I wasn't made for mountain climbing.

"We do," Finn said with a smile. "All you girls have to do is hike beside us."

"Easier said than done," Marcia said.

"Oh, and we decided we're going to do the John Muir Trail," Finn said, holding up a map.

"That means nothing to me." He could have told me we were climbing Everest, and I would have believed him. Well, not really. But they were all the same to me.

"It's a little bit longer," he started, and I groaned. "But it's also a little bit easier."

"What? How is it easier if it's longer? Maybe I don't want to do longer." Marcia groaned and pouted up at Finn.

"Trust me, if you girls haven't really hiked much, John Muir will be better."

"Okay. If you say so." I took the plate of food from him and sat down and ate. I stared at Marcia, who was sitting next to me. She had an equally nervous expression on her face. "What have we gotten ourselves into here, Marcia?"

"I don't know." She took a bite of her toast. "And I'm sorry in advance."

"Oh boy," I said, shaking my head. "I may never forgive you." I was only half joking.

"I know, but..."

"But what?"

"I'll buy you a Chanel handbag or something."

"With what money?" I started laughing, and then I looked at Finn. "Or you mean your boyfriend will buy me a Chanel handbag."

"Hey!" She poked me in the arm. "You know I don't spend my boyfriend's money." And then she paused and giggled. "Well, I try not to. I did tell you he gave me a credit card, right?" she said under her breath.

"No way. What? He trusts you with a credit card? I'm your best friend, and I definitely wouldn't give you a credit card."

"What are you two giggling about over there?" Finn said as he stopped next to Marcia's chair.

She looked up at him innocently. "Nothing."

"I think I heard something about a credit card," Brody said as he stood next to me.

"Your ears need to close," Marcia said.

He grinned down at her. "How do ears close?"

"I don't know, but if there's a way they can, yours

should." She shook her head and turned to Finn. "I was just telling Susie that you gave me a credit card, and I'm going to buy her a Chanel handbag for coming on this trip with us."

"Oh, I'll buy you ten Chanel handbags. You too, Susie. Whatever you girls want," Finn said with a grin. Then he turned toward me, a light in his eyes that had me wary. "Actually..."

"Yes?" I said suspiciously.

"There's something I want to talk to you about, Susie," Finn said.

"Oh?"

"It's about a job opening."

"No!" I said.

"Look, hear me out. I know you don't want to work for me because you feel it's some sort of nepotism. However, this is a position I think would be perfect for you."

"Hmm." I looked at Marcia. "Did you put him up to this?"

"Honestly, I didn't. I didn't even know there was a position he was considering you for."

"She didn't." He put three fingers in the air. "Scout's honor. This is something I've been thinking about, and I really think you're the right person for the role."

"Well, what's the role?"

"It would be a trainer at the company."

"What kind of trainer?"

"I know you wanted to be a substitute teacher, and you're very patient. Plus, I know you took care of all the bills and accounting for you and Marcia. Let's not talk about it now. We can talk later?"

"Okay," I said, "but only if it's because you really think I'm a good fit, and not just because I'm Marcia's best friend."

"Trust me. I don't give jobs to people because they're friends of other people I know."

"What do you mean, other people?" Marcia said, glaring at him. "I'm not just other people."

"Nope. You're my girlfriend."

"Exactly. And as such—"

"As such, you mean more to me than any other person. I love you, Marcia."

"I love you too, Finn." She leaned her head back so he could kiss her.

"Aw." Brody wrinkled his nose and pretended to stick his fingers into his mouth. "Don't tell me we're going to be dealing with you two kissing all day."

I started laughing then, and Brody and I exchanged grins.

"You girls want to finish breakfast and get ready?" Finn said as he pulled away from Marcia. "We really should start hiking in about thirty minutes."

"Okay, sounds good." Marcia and I gave each other exasperated glances. This was going to be a long, long day.

"OH MY GOSH, how many miles have we been walking?" I groaned as I fell to the ground. "I'm so tired. My legs feel like they're going to fall off."

"They're not going to fall off," Brody said with a laugh. "You're fine."

"I'm not fine. We're not even at Half Dome yet. Oh gosh, why did I agree to this? My feet are killing me."

"I'll give you a massage tonight. Make it all better."

"What does a massage have to do with my killing feet?"

He laughed. "With your killing feet?"

"You know what I mean. My brain's not even functioning right now. I meant to say my aching feet."

"I'll massage your aching feet."

"You're going to massage my feet? Really?"

He grinned, stretching his arms as if limbering up. "I'll massage your feet, your back—wherever you want."

"I suppose you'll massage my breasts as well?"

"If you want me to, I definitely wouldn't say no." He grinned.

"You're too much, Brody."

"You're the one that brought it up, Suze."

"Whatever." I shook my head. "I can't believe Marcia and Finn went ahead without us."

"You told them to. In fact, you practically begged them to keep on going while you stopped."

"Well, I didn't expect they'd actually keep going."

"I didn't keep going."

"I know. Do you want a prize for that or something?"

"Wow. You're pretty grouchy and snappy when you're tired."

"I'm more than tired, and trust me, you ain't seen nothing yet." I jumped up and stretched my arms and legs. "How much longer is it?"

"We're nearly there. I think we've got a couple more miles until we make it to the base. We show our permits, and then we get to actually ascend Half Dome." He looked at me, his eyes dark as he surveyed my face. He paused, a furrow in his brow as he seemed to be thinking. "And that's going to be the most challenging part of the hike."

"I'm already exhausted. This whole thing has been challenging."

"But isn't it beautiful?"

"It's okay," I lied as I looked around. The scenery

was stunning—absolutely stunning. I'd never been in a more beautiful place, and yet, I wasn't appreciating it as much as I should have. Not when my limbs felt like they were on fire, and I just wanted to collapse onto the ground.

"I'm going to feel like shit tomorrow," I said. "Oh my gosh. And to think I have to sleep in a sleeping bag tonight. This is gonna absolutely suck."

"You do like to complain, don't you?"

"I like to complain?" My voice rose. "You ain't seen nothing yet, Brody. Trust me."

"Well, when am I going to see the Susie monster? I'm getting a little bit nervous."

"You're laughing at me, aren't you?"

"No. Seriously, I'm not. And I understand. You're tired, and maybe you weren't prepared for this, but just try to enjoy it. It's a once-in-a-lifetime opportunity."

"I know," I said softly, "And I am enjoying it. Kind of. I'm just really tired. The most I've hiked before was three miles, and that was a lot. I didn't expect to be doing thirty or a hundred miles round trip."

"Thirty miles?" He raised an eyebrow. "Where did you get that number from?"

"Um, I was looking on Google."

"Hmm," he said. "I'm not getting reception here, but when we get back to the camp, I'm going to check. I don't think this was thirty miles."

"You want to bet?"

"Sure," he said. "What are we going to bet?"

"I don't know. Ten dollars?"

"That's nothing."

"Ten fifty?"

"No, something more than that."

"What? I don't have a job right now, so I don't really have money."

"If you looked on Google and saw the number, then you shouldn't be worried."

"Well, I'm pretty sure that was the number." I laughed. "I can't remember one hundred percent."

"Aha! How about we bet a kiss?"

"A kiss?" I stared at him for a few seconds. My body felt hot, and it wasn't from the sunshine.

"Yeah, a kiss." He took another step closer to me, and my heart started racing.

I felt like I was going to faint. I took a step back.

"What?" he asked. "Scared?"

"No. Why would I be scared? We've already kissed."

"We have, and I liked it." He took another step toward me. "I think you liked it as well, Susie Q."

"Don't call me Susie Q."

"Sorry. But am I lying?"

"No. I guess not."

"You guess not?" He started laughing. "You're the one that tried to seduce me the other night."

"I didn't try to seduce you."

"You didn't want to feel my hands on your breasts?" he said softly, looking at my lips.

"No." I shook my head. "I didn't."

"Liar." He took another step forward, and he touched my shoulder lightly. "You didn't want me to slip my fingers into your panties?"

"No!" I knew my face was bright red now. "Brody."

"Yes, Susie?"

"What are you doing?"

"I don't think I'm doing anything. I'm just stating some facts."

"They're not facts."

"I think you'll find that they are," he said. He wrapped his arm around my waist and pulled me into him. "In fact, I think..." He paused.

"Yes?"

"I think you want me to kiss you right now."

"No, I don't," I said, sputtering.

"Really?"

"Really." I nodded. "Don't."

"Don't what? I haven't even kissed you yet."

"Brody Wainwright!"

"You do love saying my name, don't you?"

"I'm just warning you."

"What, are you scared that a kiss will lead to your top coming off? And that will lead to us rolling around in the middle of the path? Are you nervous that our first time making love will be here on the John Muir Trail, where anyone could stumble upon us?

"What are you talking about?" I said, shaking my head.

"You don't want me to kiss you?"

I stared at him for a few seconds. And then, because I couldn't resist, I grabbed his head and pulled him toward me. I pressed my lips against his and kissed him hard. Then I stepped back and looked at his face. His eyes were shocked, and his fingers touched his lips. I smiled as the dazed look passed over him.

"No, I don't need you to kiss me. If I want something, I go for it." I touched my lip softly. "Now, you ready? We've got a hike to finish."

"Indeed we do," he said, and I could tell that I'd completely shocked him by the way his tone had dropped and the slight light that was in his eyes as he reappraised me. He thought he'd been dealing with some passive waif, but I was a confident woman, and I didn't mind going for what I wanted, when I wanted it.

My lips were on fire, and I wanted him to reach down and kiss me. I did want him to grab me and have his wicked way with me, but I wasn't going to tell him that. I wasn't going to tell him that I'd much rather make love to him than finish this hike.

Because there was no way I could explain to Finn and Marcia that the reason we never met them at Half Dome was because Brody and I were consummating our relationship.

TWELVE

BRODY

"So you're wearing pink panties today?" I said with a laugh as Susie marched ahead of me on the trail.

"What?" She stopped and turned around. Her eyes narrowed as she gazed at me.

"I think it's pretty self-explanatory, right? I said you're wearing pink panties today."

"And how would you know that?" she said, crossing her arms and staring at me. "Were you looking through my backpack back at camp?"

I held my hands up and shook my head quickly. "No, girl. I'm not a pervert, no matter what you think. I just saw."

"What do you mean you saw?"

"Um, you've got a hole in your pants," I said. "It's not huge, but it's big enough for me to see that you're wearing pink underwear underneath those black pants."

"Oh, no." Her hand quickly fell to her ass, and she touched around to find the hole. "Why didn't you tell me?"

"Because I only just noticed. You might remember that I've been leading most of the way, and I have a feeling that hole is new. You probably got a hole when you sat on the ground—scratched your ass on something."

"Oh, man. But yes, you're right. I do have on bright pink panties. Congratulations, you're not colorblind."

"And I'm guessing granny panties, huh?"

"Excuse me?"

"I'm just saying. They're covering your ass cheek. If you were wearing a thong, I would've seen your flesh. But seeing as I'm not, you're wearing granny panties."

"I think I've had enough of this conversation, thank you very much," she said. "Are we continuing?"

"Yeah, we're continuing." I laughed, and she started walking again.

We walked in companionable silence, and I could tell she was feeling tired. "You want something to drink?"

"No, I'm okay. Thank you."

"You want to stop for a little bit?"

"I do want to stop for a lot of bit," she said, rolling her eyes. "But we should keep on. We still have the hardest part of the trek to go, right?"

"Yeah, but look. If we get to Half Dome, and you don't want to go up the cables, we don't have to."

"But isn't that the most intense part?"

"Exactly. It is."

"But isn't that also the part that has the best view?"

"Um, yeah, kind of. At least, from photos, it looks like it."

"Oh, you've never been before?"

"No. I've been to Yosemite before, but I've never climbed Half Dome. I used to think I'd like to go rock climbing here, but..." I paused. "Well, obviously, it didn't happen."

"I didn't know you were a rock climber. Do you go often?"

"Not anymore," I shook my head, not wanting to get into this conversation.

"I'm kind of scared of heights," she said. "So I don't think I'd ever go rock climbing. I did try once in college—Marcia and I went. There was a guy she liked." She made a face, and I laughed.

"So you went rock climbing because of a guy?"

"Well, no. I went rock climbing because of Marcia, and Marcia went rock climbing because of this guy that she liked. And let's just say, we both got stuck halfway up."

"Seriously?"

"Yeah, and it was only a twelve-foot wall. So that tells you how much we like heights."

"Interesting," I said. "I guess I now know not to take you rock climbing."

"Well, you're not going to take me anywhere, are you?" she said, giving me a look.

"I don't know." I shrugged. "Maybe I will. Maybe I won't."

"It's not just up to you, right? I would have to agree to it."

"You're telling me you wouldn't agree to a date with me?"

"A date? Since when were we talking about a date?"

"Why else would you be going with me somewhere?"

"Because we're friends, or becoming friends."

"True, but I don't really do the friend thing."

"Oh, you only do the fuck them thing?"

I stared at her, my eyebrows raising at her words. My heart raced slightly, and I felt my lips twitching as I stared at the indignant look on her face. "I didn't think you used such language, Susie."

"What, fuck?"

I nodded. "Yeah. You always seem..."

"Please don't tell me I seem like a delicate flower. We both know I'm not."

"True, there is nothing delicate about you at night when you're snoring."

"I do not snore," she said, hitting me in the shoulder.

"Yeah, you do." I nodded. "I'm surprised no one's told you that."

"I don't snore. I..."

"You what?"

"Nothing." She glared at me. "You snore too, you know."

"Oh, really?" I said with a smile. "You were listening to me snore?"

"Well, you kind of woke me up."

"Liar," I said. "You were in a deep sleep."

"No, I wasn't." And then she laughed. "Okay, maybe last night I was in a deep sleep. But the previous night, I wasn't. And you snored."

"Was it loud?"

"No," she said. "It was okay."

"Your snoring was okay too. When you sleep, your face is all soft and still. Definitely like a delicate flower. Maybe a rose or a lily or a—"

"Oh my gosh," she groaned.

"What? It's not like I'm quoting Shakespeare."

"Don't tell me you're the sort of guy that quotes Shakespeare on dates."

"Why? Would that be so bad?"

"That would be absolutely awful."

I pointed ahead of us. "Look. You see? There's Marcia and Finn waiting for us."

"We made it. I didn't think it would happen." She held her hands up in the air. "I did it. I did it. I made it."

"Um, not so fast, Susie. We haven't finished the hike yet."

"Well. I mean, kind of, right?"

"No." I shook my head. "You see over there?" I pointed to the large flat-faced rock to the left of us.

"What the hell is that?"

"That's Half Dome." I grinned. "That's what we have to climb next."

She gasped. "Holy shit. There's no way. There's absolutely no way. My legs feel like they're going to fall off. I can't climb up there. Look at the cables. It's literally cables and pieces of wood against a flat rock. How the hell?"

"I'll be by your side," I said softly. "Every step of the way. I got you, Susie."

She stared at me for a few seconds, not saying anything. And then she smiled. "I was kind of wrong about you, I guess."

"What do you mean?"

"There's a gentleman in there after all. A kind soul. Never would've thought that a jock could be so thoughtful and considerate."

"All jocks aren't bad, you know?"

"True," she said. "I guess I haven't met any that were good before."

"You have to remember that I haven't always been a jock. Maybe that's the difference."

"Maybe. And Brody?"

"Yeah?" I said, wondering what she was going to say next.

"If you dare tell Finn or Marcia that I kissed you, I will do some unspeakable things to you tonight." Her lips twitched and she winked.

Flabbergasted, I stared at her for a few seconds as she went running off to Marcia. There was something so different about Susie. So unexpected. I never knew what was going to come out of her mouth. I never knew what she was going to say or do. And I found that I quite liked it. I found that I liked that I didn't know what she was going to say next. She was different to every other woman I'd met. And well, it surprised me.

I'd never felt that way about a woman before. I'd never felt challenged or excited or just wanted to spend time with them. Susie was someone special, and it was a pity that she was so closely connected to my friend group. As much as I liked her, I couldn't let anything else happen between us, because I was a man that could never give more of myself than I already did.

THIRTEEN

SUSIE

My legs were burning, and I felt like I was a soldier in an army as we made our way back to camp. It was now past nine p.m., the sunlight had long gone, and I knew I was ready to drop to the ground.

"You okay, Susie?" Brody walked by my side, and I just nodded my response. "Want more water?"

"No, thanks."

"You did awesome today."

"I feel like I'm going to die." I sighed. "Next time someone asks me to go climb a mountain, I'm going to say no."

"Aw, maybe just a little bit of training next time?"

"There will not be a next time."

"For me either." Marcia moaned in front of us. "Finn, you're lucky I'm even still dating you."

"It wasn't that bad, was it?" Finn sounded chipper and happy, and I just glared at his back.

"Quit while you're ahead, dude." Brody laughed. "So, anymore stories to tell us, Susie?"

"Nope."

"Ooh, why don't you tell us your sexy story?" Marcia grinned at me wickedly, and I shook my head. I was definitely going to kill her when I had more energy.

"Sexy story?" Brody looked at me with a raised eyebrow.

"Yeah." I shrugged. "I was writing a steamy romance book, but I didn't get far."

"How steamy?" He grinned.

I laughed. "Not that steamy."

Marcia spoke up again. "It was when she had a crush on her boyfriend's dad."

I couldn't believe she was sharing all my secrets.

"You don't have a boyfriend now right?" Brody questioned me and I sighed.

"No, I don't. This was a guy I dated in college for like a month. I met his dad at a football game, I thought he was hot, and it gave me an idea for a book."

"Do tell more." Brody sounded intrigued, and I realized that he was really interested in hearing it.

"It was stupid, and I didn't get very far."

"Tell us," Finn chimed in.

"You guys are so goofy. But if you really want to hear it..."

"I really do," Brody said. "I knew you had to be a writer."

"I'm not a writer. I've never published anything."

"Well, I'm sure you will soon."

"Unlikely," I said, though secretly, I hoped his words would come true. I'd never admitted out loud to anyone how badly I wanted to be published. It was a dream that I never thought would come true.

"So are you going to read some of this book to us then?" Brody asked hopefully, and I smiled at his eagerness.

"Fine." I grinned. "Hold on." I cleared my throat and thought back to the beginning of the story I'd written. I was slightly nervous to recite it to them. It was slightly scandalous, but I realized I didn't care. I pulled out my phone and opened Google Docs to search for the file, and then I began reading.

THE FIRST TIME we met was not like a fairy tale. I could remember it clearly. He was standing to the side of the room, a crystal goblet filled with honey-brown whiskey in his hand. He was wearing a navy blue suit, with a darker blue silk tie. His eyes were a smoldery gray, and the gold cufflinks on the sides of his shirt cuffs sparkled in the bright light directly above him.

I held the tray of canapés in my right hand and looked around the smoky room to see if anyone wanted one. All of the men were ignoring me—except him. He signaled me over to him as if I were his own personal servant, and I went because I didn't want to lose my job. I had one more semester of college to go before I could get out of this town, and the less debt I had, the better.

"A thousand dollars."

Those were the only words he spoke to me. I stared at him for a few seconds, not sure what he was saying. He placed the decanter on the table next to him and took a step toward me. His right hand touched my waist and slid down until it was on my ass. I should have hit it away, but I quite liked how forward he was being. I suppose I was so used to being with boys that didn't know I'd even like a dominant man.

"A thousand dollars," he said again; this time, in a lower

voice. He squeezed my ass, rubbing against my thong. I stared up at him, not quite believing what I was hearing. He pulled his wallet out of his pocket and counted out ten crisp one-hundred-dollar bills before placing them next to the decanter. He nodded to a door behind him. I handed him my tray and walked to the door. I felt like I was in a trance. I opened the door and found myself in a study.

"What are you doing, Cassie?" I whispered to myself as I slid my panties off and smoothed my dress back down. I hurried back out of the room and saw that he was standing there, still as could be. He didn't even turn to look at me as I exited the room.

I grabbed the tray of canapés and stopped in front of him. His green eyes mocked me as I handed him the panties, and he slipped them into his jacket pocket and then walked away. I stared after him, my face bright red. I was embarrassed and ashamed. I grabbed the money and tucked it into my bra. One thousand dollars for my panties. I tried to convince myself that it was a story I'd laugh about when I got older and that it was unlikely I'd ever see him again. I was wrong.

The second time we met, it was like a nightmare. It was supposed to be a cute meet-the-parents night. My boyfriend of three months, Daniel King, was the sweetest guy I'd ever met, and when he'd asked me to meet his parents, I'd been more than happy to say yes—even if I knew the relationship wasn't going anywhere.

I sensed something was wrong as soon as I entered the house. It was as if his presence charged every location he filled. When I saw him standing in the corner of the living room, his back to me, I knew it was him. I could feel my throat constricting as Daniel grabbed my hand and brought me closer and closer to him.

"Dad, I want you to meet someone."

And when he turned around and his eyes met mine, he didn't even look surprised. I wondered if he knew who I was. Perhaps he'd forgotten about me. There was nothing in his expression to make me think he hadn't. He reached his hand out to me and shook it as if I were a stranger. Which I guess, in some sense, I was.

And then Daniel went off to get us drinks, and it was just the two of us. I smiled at him pleasantly, about to ask him about his day, when he took a step toward me and looked down at me with his gray eyes.

"One million dollars."

He didn't blink as I gasped. I stared at him in shock. This time, I wasn't sure what he wanted. This time, he was offering more money than I'd ever thought I'd have in my life.

"One million dollars, and I don't tell my son who you really are."

I STOPPED THEN and waited for someone to say something. I was nervous they would absolutely hate it.

Marcia groaned. "Susie, please tell me you're not stopping there. I want to know more."

"I, too, am intrigued," Finn said and I laughed, feeling delirious.

"Why did you stop?" Brody grabbed my arm. "What does she have to do for the million dollars?"

"I haven't decided yet." All of a sudden, I felt happy and full of energy. "Did you guys really like it?"

"It was amazing, Susie." Marcia was excited too. "I can't

believe I've never heard this before. When did you write it?"

"A while ago." I was beaming in the night air, and I didn't even care that we were still on our descent back to the campground.

"Oh, look." Finn stopped and pointed to the right. "That's the campground. We've completed our hike." He grinned at all of us. "Thanks so much for coming with me guys. It has been the most amazing day."

FOURTEEN

BRODY

"Hey, Finn. I think these girls are in bad shape," I whispered to Finn as we stood at the edge of the campsite. Marcia and Susie were sitting on the camp chairs moaning. I could see that Susie's calf muscles were spasming, and Marcia had thrown up. "I don't think we should stay at the campsite tonight."

"You're right," Finn said. "I feel absolutely awful. I shouldn't have made them do the hike. I should've known it would be too much for them."

"It's okay. They enjoyed it, but I don't think they'll enjoy the night if they have to sleep in a sleeping bag on the ground."

"I think there are a couple of hotels close to here." He looked at his watch. "It's kind of late, so I'm not sure what will be open."

"Do you want to make some calls, and I'll start packing up the tents?"

"Do you think we should start packing them up before we find a place to go?" he asked.

"Yeah." I nodded. "Even if we have to drive a little farther, we can't let these girls sleep in these tents, dude."

"You're right." He stared at me for a few seconds and chuckled. "I never thought I'd see the day."

"What?" I said.

"When Brody Wainwright was so considerate of other people's feelings."

"I've always been considerate of other people's feelings. I mean, okay. Maybe not always. But Marcia is your girlfriend, and I assume she's going to be your wife one day. And, well... Susie's a cool chick."

"I'm glad you see that." Finn nodded, though there was a twinkle in his eye that told me there was something else on his mind.

"Yeah, I do. And she's a pretty awesome storyteller as well."

"She really is," Finn said. He looked at me knowingly and grinned widely, and I wondered what he was thinking about.

"What is it, dude?"

"Well, you know I was about to buy that publishing house, right?"

"Oh, yeah. I remember you mentioned something about it. So, what? You're going to offer her a deal or something?"

"I would, but she wouldn't take it. I know her. She's prideful and wants to make it on her own. And I respect that, but she's got talent."

"She really does." I nodded. "Shit, if I were to ever write a biography, she'd be my ghostwriter."

"Then you wouldn't be writing it, dude."

"And that's the point." I laughed. "But anyway, go make those calls. I'll check on the girls."

"Sounds good."

I walked over to Marcia and Susie and kneeled down next to them. "You guys okay? Finn's going to see if we can find a hotel reservation for the night so we don't have to sleep in these tents."

"Really?" Marcia looked hopeful. "Because I really don't want to sleep in that sleeping bag again tonight."

"Me neither," Susie groaned. "It was a pretty sight and all, but my entire body feels like it belongs to someone else."

"Don't worry. We'll figure something out." I jumped up. "As long as you're hydrated, right?" They both nodded. "Okay, I'm going to disassemble these tents and roll up the sleeping bags so everything's ready for when Finn finds us a place. You just sit there, okay?"

"Okay. Thanks, Brody." Susie's voice sounded surprisingly chill.

"No worries," I said. I walked away and started folding up the tent. "So, do you want to tell me another story, Susie? I'm in the mood to hear something sexy."

"Oh my gosh." Marcia said.

"What? You liked her previous story too," I defended.

"Yeah, but it was sexy in the things that she didn't say, not in the things that she did say."

"Well, isn't that always what's sexiest?" I said as I took the poles out of the first tent. "The tease and the chase are always so much fun."

"Isn't it just?" Susie said, shaking her head.

"Hey, did I hit a nerve there?"

"No, but I feel like guys are always all about the chase," Susie said. "And then once they have you, they no longer want you."

"That's not true," I said. "Well, not for every guy."

"Is it true for you?" Marcia asked me pointedly.

"That's not a fair question. I don't actually chase women."

"Oh, let me guess..." Susie started laughing. "They chase you, huh?"

"Well, what can I say? I'm—"

"Brody Wainwright," they chorused together, and we all laughed.

"Hey, what's so funny?" Finn said as he walked back into the campsite.

"Nothing. Any luck?"

"Yeah, actually. I was able to find us two rooms. However..." He paused and looked at the two women.

"What?" Marcia said.

"They're king-sized beds."

"Okay. That works," Susie said. "Me and Marcia and you and Brody."

"I was kind of hoping to be with Marcia," Finn said quickly. "But, I mean, obviously if you don't feel comfortable sleeping in a bed with Brody..."

"I'll be a gentleman." I held my hand up. "I promise. You don't have to worry about me, Susie."

She stared at me.

"In fact, if anyone was worried about losing their honor, it would be me. I don't know what you're going to try and do."

"What I'm going to try and do?" She started laughing. "Are you joking me?"

"Hey, I might wake up in the middle of the night with you on top of me."

"I don't think so." She shook her head. "Especially not the way my muscles are feeling."

"So if your muscles were feeling good, it'd be a possibility?"

"No, it would not," she shouted.

Marcia shook her head. "I can sleep with you, Susie, if you really don't feel comfortable with Brody."

"I'm right here," I said, feeling pissed off. My voice rose as I tapped my hand against my thigh. "What do you think I'm going to do? What sort of man do you think I am? I can be a gentleman, you know."

"Really?" Susie said.

"Yeah. Did I do anything in the tent with you for the last couple of nights?"

"I guess not," she said, blushing.

I was pretty sure things could've gotten a lot further if I'd pushed a little harder, but I had a feeling she hadn't told Marcia that.

"It's fine," Susie said. "Marcia, you can be with Finn. I know you probably want to hug and kiss and whatever. Plus, Brody said he'll massage my calves."

"And your feet and your shoulders and whatever else you want."

"There will be nothing else I want you to massage, thank you very much," she said.

"Okay. If you say so."

"I am saying so."

"Let me help you finish up there," Finn said as he headed toward me. "Girls, if you want to go and get in the car, we should be all packed up within the next couple of minutes."

"Sounds good," Marcia said as she stood up. She and Susie headed toward the truck, and I watched them for a few seconds.

"Dude, don't be getting any ideas," Finn said.

"Me?" I said innocently. "What ideas could I possibly have?"

"WOW, this hotel room is absolutely beautiful," Susie said as she sat on the king-sized bed. She looked around the room, her eyes appreciative and happy. "And this mattress—oh, it's so soft," she said as she lay back.

I stared down at her, a wry smile on my face. I'd never seen her looking so ecstatic. I liked that look on her face.

"It's pretty nice," I said, nodding. A hotel room was a hotel room to me.

She sat up suddenly. "I'm going to go take a shower because I feel dirty and grimy, and I'm hoping the hot water will help my muscles."

"Okay." I nodded. "When you get out of the shower, don't put too many clothes on."

"Excuse me?" She blinked at me. "What?"

"If I'm going to massage you, it'll be a lot easier if you're not wearing much clothing."

"Oh. Yeah, sure," she said. "You really don't have to massage me, Brody."

"No, trust me. It will make you feel better tomorrow morning if you relax those muscles tonight."

"Okay. I guess I'll wear some shorts and a T-shirt. Does that work?"

"Yeah. And put on your bra and panties too."

"Of course I'm going to put on my bra and panties."

"Well, I'm just saying. You might need to take off your shorts and T-shirt."

"Excuse me?"

"It's going to be kind of hard for me to massage your back if you have a T-shirt on. Don't worry. I'm not going to make you turn over."

"Uh-huh. Sure you're not."

"I'm not," I said. "Like I said, I can be a gentleman."

"If you say so."

I grinned at her and watched as she walked to the shower. She was sexy. And if she weren't so tired and achy, I would definitely try something with her. But I didn't want her to regret it in the morning.

It was weird, me thinking that, because I'd never really worried about how a woman was going to feel in the morning. As long as she consented to whatever we had planned, I'd been okay with it. It's not like I'd ever lied to a woman or told her that we were going to have a relationship or that sex was going somewhere. Most of the women I hooked up with knew the deal. But I had a feeling Susie was different. I had a feeling Susie wasn't the sort of woman that slept with men just to sleep with them.

It wasn't that she was completely innocent. Her story had made me hard, and I had a feeling she had a kinky, dirty side to her that she hadn't even explored yet. A part of me wanted to be the man that she explored it with, but I knew Finn would kill me. And maybe Marcia too.

But Susie seemed the sort that would definitely be down to try whips and handcuffs and pinwheels and all sorts of other accoutrements one could find at a sex store.

I groaned as I realized I was thinking about her in a physical and intimate way. I had to get those thoughts out of my mind. There would be nothing worse than me being hard while giving her a massage. She'd definitely be able to feel it against her. And while normally I wasn't against a woman knowing how aroused I was, I didn't want Susie to feel uncomfortable.

I liked her. I really liked her as much more than a sex object. She was someone I could see myself becoming friends with—if I didn't want to fuck her.

But I did want to fuck her, so it was unlikely that I'd pursue any sort of real friendship with her. That would just make things complicated. And as I was a man, I knew my head down below would often win out above my head above. And, well, my head down below wanted to get to know her much more intimately, and that wouldn't be a good idea for either of us.

FIFTEEN

SUSIE

Brody was lying on the bed with his shirt off and his eyes closed as I exited the bathroom. I stood by the doorway and just stared at him for a few seconds. He was handsome, and his chest was perfection—a deep tan and sprinkled with dark hair.

I crept forward, holding the towel that was wrapped around my hair in place so that it didn't fall to the ground. I didn't want to wake Brody. I swallowed hard as I realized just how attracted to him I was. His wavy, dark hair against the white pillow made me want to run my fingers through his tresses, and my mouth went dry as I stared at his handsome face.

I would never admit it to anyone, but I understood why women fell for him. Shit, I even understood why women dropped their panties for him after one glance. He was sexy. And based on the way he'd kissed me, he knew how to turn a woman on.

"Like what you see?" His deep voice was teasing as he sat up and rubbed his eyes. "Sorry, I guess I was more tired than I thought."

"That's okay. You should sleep."

"But I promised you a massage." His eyes narrowed as he looked me over from head to foot. I trembled slightly under his gaze. He shifted on the bed and ran his hands through his hair as his smile spread. "A gentleman always follows through on his offers."

"Uh-huh," I said as I sat on the edge of the bed. My boy shorts rode up so that my thighs were almost completely exposed, and my nipples pushed against the thin material of my shirt. I hadn't bothered to put on a bra. But he didn't have to know that.

"Shall we start, then?" He moved over on the bed and patted the mattress. "Lie down on your stomach."

I stared at the mattress and then at him. All of a sudden, this didn't seem like the smartest idea, and I normally prided myself on making good decisions.

"Relax, Susie." Brody's voice was calming. "I want you to enjoy this massage."

"I want to enjoy it as well, but..." I paused, not really knowing what to say next.

"But what?" he said, a concerned tone in his voice.

"I just don't want you to think that this is going somewhere it's not."

"Don't worry. I'm not going to seduce you unless you want me to."

"Is everything a joke to you, Brody?" I said, perplexed.

"No. Why would you say that?" I could hear the humor in his voice, but there was also a tinge of something else. Something that resembled regret. I wondered if I was just imagining that emotion.

"Because you always seem to resort to making everything a joke. Sometimes people are serious."

"Trust me, Susie. I can be very serious. If you've ever seen me play baseball, you'd know that."

"Well, I'm glad you can be serious about baseball, but what about everything else in life?"

"Whoa, you sound like my ex-girlfriend," he said. "What have I done to upset you?"

"I'm not saying you upset me, and frankly, I'm surprised you even have an ex-girlfriend."

"I guess I don't really consider her an ex-girlfriend. She was more of a friend with benefits. But that's what the argument was about."

"What?" I wanted to turn around, but I realized that wouldn't be a good idea.

"She thought she was my girlfriend, so when she caught me banging her best friend, she kind of got upset."

"Oh my gosh, you're such a dog."

"No, I'm honest. I like sex, and I like women who like sex, and I like to have fun. She wasn't my girlfriend."

"You slept with her best friend, though. That's crude. That's—"

"I know, I know. But shouldn't it have been the best friend that said no? Didn't the best friend owe her allegiance more than me?"

"You say potato, I say potahto." I rolled my eyes, and he rolled his eyes back at me in a mocking fashion. He shifted on the mattress so that he was closer to me, and I could see the unruly curls at the front of his face were tinged with blond.

"I'm not trying to get you upset, Susie."

"Why did you even bring it up, then? You can't think I'd love to hear that fact about you. You can't think that would make you go up in my esteem."

"Who says I want to go up in your esteem?"

"Well, fine. Maybe you don't. Just give me my massage. Whatever."

"You sound stressed." He sighed, and his voice lowered. "I didn't mean to make you upset. I just wanted to help you relax"

"Just give me the massage. It's okay, Brody. I shouldn't expect more from you than you're willing to give."

"What are you expecting from me? What are you hoping to expect from me? I'm confused."

"Nothing," I said, though I didn't want to tell him that I thought we'd be getting closer. I didn't want to tell him that I was attracted to him for both his body and his mind. I didn't want to tell him that I thought he was a thoughtful, sweet guy that was frankly pained about something, because I knew I sounded like every other stupid woman out there that thought she could change a man who had issues and was a commitment-phobe.

He and I had nothing. We'd barely kissed. We'd certainly never slept together. And just because I felt like I wanted to—well, my body knew it wanted to, but that was another story—it didn't mean we were closer than we actually were.

His hands were on my shoulders, and I sighed as he squeezed.

"Is it okay?" he said softly.

"It feels nice. Thank you. You really didn't have to."

"I wanted to. I know that I can be a bit of a joker sometimes, but I care about my friends. And I do consider you a friend. A new friend, but a friend. I mean, we've shared a tent together now."

"Yeah, we have. At least it wasn't a sleeping bag," I said, half-joking.

"That would've been something, eh?" he said softly. "If

I would've made more of a move when we were in the tent, would you have shared one with me?"

"I don't think you should be asking me this question when I'm half-naked," I said, sighing as his thumbs pressed into my spine. A massage was exactly what I needed. It felt absolutely magnificent, and I relaxed under his touch.

"I think this is the perfect time."

"I feel like I could fall asleep," I said softly. "Tell me a story so I don't."

"Tell you a story? I'm not you. I don't have a way with words like you do."

"I'm sure you do, Brody. I'm sure you have plenty of stories. Tell me about baseball, or tell me about what it was like being a nerd in high school."

"Wow, you really want to get deep, huh? Are you some sort of shrink?"

"No, I'm not. Which I think is quite obvious. I'd have a lot more patience if I was."

"True," he said. "You would."

"What are you trying to say?" I laughed. "You don't think I'm patient?"

"Not really. But I like you, so it's okay."

"Well..." I said after a few seconds, not really knowing how to respond to his admission of liking me. "What are you going to tell me?"

"Do you want me to tell you a fairy tale? Once upon a time in a land far, far away..." he started.

"Come on, Brody."

"Okay, you want a personal story, then."

"That would be nice."

"Let me think," he said as his hands moved closer to my lower back. I arched slightly and sighed as his fingers dug into my flesh.

"So, I know," he said softly. "Once—"

"Oh gosh, not again."

"What? All I said was 'once.'"

"Was it going to be once upon a time?"

"Actually, no, it wasn't. It was going to be: once when I was younger."

"Okay, continue."

"Well, thank you, Miss Susie."

"You're welcome, Mr. Brody."

"Mr. Brody? Why does that make me sound like an old man?"

"I don't know, but stop changing the subjects. I want to hear more."

"Fine," he said. "When I was younger, my brothers and I liked to pretend we were knights."

"Knights? Like knights of the round table sort of knights?"

"Yeah," he said. "I guess every young boy likes to pretend he's a prince or a knight or a king."

"I guess I did pretend I was a princess. Never a queen, though."

"Ah, but you are a princess, Susie."

"Oh, my. Enough with the flattery, Brody. Continue with your story, please."

"Fine," he said. "Well, I remember we were at my grandparents' farm."

"In Kentucky, right?"

"Yeah. Good memory."

"Yeah, I do remember small things," I said. "So you were at your grandparents' farm in Kentucky."

"Yeah, and there was a neighbor girl. She didn't live there. She was actually visiting her grandparents too. I remember her because she was stunningly beautiful. She had long blonde hair and big blue eyes. She was possibly the most beautiful girl I'd ever seen in my life."

As I listened to him, I could feel twists and turns of jealousy in my gut. I didn't know why I cared so much, but hearing him talk about this woman with the long blonde hair and blue eyes...

Jealousy was so very opposite to me, and I didn't want him to know. I didn't want to feel insecure. It wasn't like she and I were in any sort of competition.

"So she was your princess?" I said.

"No," he said with a chuckle. "She was my damsel in distress. I wasn't the only one that thought she was pretty. Both of my brothers did."

"You're the middle child, right?"

"Yeah. You really listen well."

"I try," I said. "So you and your brothers both liked her?"

"Yeah, and it became our mission to see which one of us she liked."

"Oh."

"So we were knights of the round table," he said, "and we were going to have a duel—a fight to the death for the hand of the fair maiden."

"What was her name?" I said softly. I wondered where she was now, if she was married and had a happy family. All the things I wish I had but didn't.

"Honestly?" He laughed. "I can't even remember."

"You can't remember? She was the most beautiful woman you'd ever seen in your life."

"Well, she wasn't a woman. She was a girl. I was just a mere boy at the time."

"Still, you can't remember her name."

"It wasn't that serious, Susie. Trust me. That summer, it was serious, but not in the grand scheme of things."

"I guess," I said.

"Do you want me to continue the story or not?"

"I do, I do. Please continue."

"So anyway, one day we decided to have a duel on some of our horses."

"Oh, your grandparents had horses?"

"Yeah," he said. "They loved horses. Grams grew up on a horse farm, and so she was never without a horse by her side." He sounded thoughtful. "Sometimes Gramps used to say she loved the horses more than him, but it wasn't true of course. She doted on Gramps. If he would've seen the way she looked at him..." He paused. "Well, that was true love."

"Aw, are they still alive?" I said.

"No." His answer was abrupt. "But anyway, I'm drifting from the story. I told you I wasn't good at this."

"You're fine, Brody. I want to hear more."

"So one day, we decided we'd have a three-way duel."

"How does that work? Isn't a duel between two people?"

"Yes, but we were young country boys. We decided that the three of us would all ride horses with handmade spears from long branches of wood, and whoever got knocked off was out. The last man standing, or rather sitting on his horse, was the winner."

"I guess that makes sense. So who won the fair damsel's hand?"

"Wouldn't you know it? None of us."

"None of you? What? You all fell off?" I asked.

"No." He laughed. "My older brother won, or rather he was the last one on the horse, and he went to go and claim her hand. And do you know what she said?"

"No, obviously not. What did she say? Wait, let me guess. She said she wanted you instead."

"No. She said violence was never the answer, and that a fight was never the way to win a woman's heart. That we were trying to make the decision for her, and if any of us had actually really liked her, we would've come to her first and asked her what her wishes were."

"Wow. Profound," I said. "I'm impressed."

"Well, now I understand. But at the time, we were absolutely flabbergasted."

"So what did you do?"

"We all went and got ice cream, of course. I remember thinking that I'd gotten all those bruises for nothing."

"Oh, no. Were you seriously hurt?"

"Not really. I think my pride was more than anything. You see, I'd come up with a calculation that was meant to help me win."

"A calculation?"

"Well, an angle, so to speak. Remember, I dealt with math and angles and physics, and I came up with a strategy that was meant to help me win. I was going to approach from a forty-five-degree angle with my spear at a seventy-degree angle and—"

"You're absolutely losing me."

"Sorry," he said. "But I was more disappointed by the fact that my calculations were wrong. I didn't account for the fact that brutal strength meant so much more than my calculations."

"I guess many people don't account for that fact," I said with a laugh.

"I don't forget it now," he said. "Is the massage okay?"

"It's been wonderful. Thank you." And I turned over

because I wanted to see his face. His eyes went wide as I grabbed the towel and pulled it up to cover my breasts.

"You want me to massage somewhere else?" he asked with a wicked little grin."

"No." I smiled up at him. "I knew you would think that, though."

"A man can only hope."

I grabbed his neck and pulled him toward me before kissing him hard. He kissed me back passionately. And as he massaged my scalp and played with my hair, I opened my mouth wider.

His fingers slipped up under my shirt, and I didn't stop him. His touch was magic, and his story had made me feel closer to him—made me feel like I knew a little part of him that no one else did. I was almost positive this wasn't a story he'd shared with anyone else, because Brody was not a sharer. His entire persona was one of nonchalance and care-freeness, and this was a story from the heart.

I moaned as his fingers found my nipples, and he pinched them tightly. He kissed me passionately, and I kissed him back.

"You are so sexy, Susie," he said.

"You're pretty sexy yourself," I said as his fingers reached down and slipped into my panties. I parted my legs, unable to think straight as he brushed me, gently at first and then with more intent. I moaned as he touched my wetness, and he groaned against my lips.

"Fuck, you're wet." He kissed down the valley between my breasts to my stomach, and he kissed my belly button and sucked. I cried out as his teeth fell to the top of my panties and pulled them down quickly.

He looked into my eyes, and I nodded slightly as he pulled them off my feet. He spread my legs, and before I knew what was happening, his tongue was between my legs and he was licking me, teasing me, making me cry out and beg him to continue. I didn't know which way was up or down. All I knew was that this was the most sensual I've felt in years.

As his tongue entered me, I gripped his shoulders and dug my fingernails into him. This seemed to encourage him, because he started fucking me with his tongue even harder before sucking on my clit. I cried out as my arms flew out and my fingers gripped the sheets. He looked up at me with a wicked grin.

"Come for me, Susie. Come for me," he said. And before I knew what was happening, my body was shaking and I was exploding. He licked up every drop and then kissed back up my body before landing on my lips. His hands were on the sides of my face as he kissed me on the nose and then the forehead.

"Well, I'll say that was a massage worth remembering, huh?" He winked at me and pulled me into his arms. And I just grinned back at him, not knowing what else to say or do.

I nodded as he jumped up out of the bed and turned off the light and came back to me. I half expected that he would try to make love to me, but he didn't. That surprised me. He seemed like the sort of guy that would go for it if he thought he had a chance, and he had a very good chance of making love with me. In this moment, I would deny him nothing, but he didn't even pursue it.

I touched him on the shoulder and then reached down to his pants. I rubbed against his cock hard, and he groaned.

"Don't, Susie," he said softly.

"Why not?" I said teasingly, seductively, as my fingers

played with the head of his cock. He groaned and shifted so that he was gyrating against my hand.

"Because if you touch me, this night will go down a path I don't think you want it to."

"What path is that?"

"I will have you on all fours, and I'll be fucking you from behind so good and hard that you'll never forget the feel of my cock inside of you."

I shivered as I listened to his words. "But I don't think you want that, Susie. Not yet." He pulled me against him and kissed me. "Let's sleep. We have a long day ahead of us tomorrow."

I kissed him back, then buried my head into his shoulder and closed my eyes as I stroked his chest.

He was right, of course. If I slept with him, I'd never be able to forget it. And if we were going to be in each other's lives due to our best friends being together, then it was better that I didn't put myself in that position. I didn't want to make things awkward for any of us.

SIXTEEN
BRODY

I could hear Susie humming from the bathroom as I opened my eyes. I lay in the bed and stared up at the ceiling, remembering the previous night. It had been the first time in a long time that I'd actually walked away from sex. I'd been so hard and had wanted her so badly, but I'd had to put our friendship over my carnal needs.

She walked out of the shower, a towel around her hair, and she grinned at me.

"Morning, Wainwright."

"Morning, Susie," I said. "Why the last name?"

"I don't know. I figured that's what your teammates call you, right?"

"Um, my teammates do call me Wainwright, but you're not my teammate."

"So you're saying you'd rather I call you Brody?"

"I do think it's appropriate," I said as I jumped out of the bed. I grabbed her hand and pulled her toward me. "Morning," I said, giving her a big kiss.

Her eyes widened in surprise, and I grinned.

"So, last night was fun," I said.

"Yeah, it was." She smiled back at me, her brown eyes staring innocently into mine.

"You wanted me so badly, didn't you?"

"I think *you* wanted *me*. Did I give you blue balls?" she said, and I laughed.

She was fun, and she didn't take herself too seriously.

"Honestly, you did give me blue balls, and I think I'm about to go into the shower and take care of a little something something before we go to breakfast with Finn and Marcia. I don't want them thinking I'm getting frisky with you at the table."

"What do you mean?" she said. "Frisky?"

"Because there are certain things I'd like to do to you."

"You wouldn't try anything at breakfast," she said, disbelief in her tone.

"You want to bet?"

She narrowed her eyes at me.

"I can show you if you really want to know," I said, staring at her, hoping she would say yes. I'd love to play with her at the breakfast table. I'd love to have her mouth opening and gasping and having everyone wondering what's going on.

"No," she said, shaking her head. "I believe you."

"Smart girl. I guess you don't want to be played with under the table."

"Does anyone want to be played with under the table? Actually, don't answer that," she said, shaking her head. "So you're going to go into the shower now?"

"I think I am." I nodded. I stared at her for a few seconds and then looked at my watch. "However, if you want a quick fuck, we can…"

"Really, Brody?" She looked disappointed.

"What? I'm just offering."

"I really thought we had a good time last night, and I thought you were going to stop being—"

"Stop being me?"

"If you mean being a jerk, yeah."

"I'm just who I am. Take it or leave it," I said and licked my lips.

"You know what? Let's pretend you didn't just say that. You go shower, and I'll call Marcia and see when they're ready for breakfast."

"Sounds good to me." I could feel my spirits lowering.

I'd ruined the mood that had been so light and fun. I shouldn't have asked her if she wanted to fuck, but it was my way of diffusing the situation. It had felt almost too comfortable between us, and while I liked it, I didn't want that feeling. I didn't want to feel domesticated. I didn't want to feel like there was something special between us, because I wasn't looking for that with anyone.

I walked into the bathroom and turned on the shower. The water was slightly cool. Susie must have taken a long shower for all the hot water to have been gone already. I closed my eyes and leaned back and thought about the taste of her from the previous night and the way she'd held my head against her so she could feel my tongue deeper inside of her.

I thought about the way her breasts had jiggled, and the way her back had arched as I'd played with her nipples. My hand soon found its way to my cock, and I jacked off quickly, shuddering in the shower as I had one of the most intense orgasms I'd had in a long time.

My eyes flew open as I realized that was due to the thought of Susie. She was in my head constantly, and I didn't like how much I was attracted to her. I didn't like how much I wanted to be with her.

I quickly shampooed my hair and got out of the shower and walked into the room. I was disappointed to see that Susie was not there. I pulled on my clothes and grabbed my phone and exited. I headed down to the lobby and toward the dining room. Susie sat there with Marcia, having an intense conversation about something. Finn was standing behind Marcia's chair, and they all looked up as I entered the room.

"Morning," I said. "How's everyone doing today?"

"I'm sore as hell," Marcia said, grimacing.

"Me too," Susie said. "I thought the shower would help a little bit, but my bones and muscles and every part of my body feels super weary."

"Really?" I said, surprised. "Even after, you know..." I winked to her.

"I don't know what you're talking about," she said, her face turning slightly pink.

"You know, even after I went down on you, and you screamed out my name?"

"Brody." She jumped up and hit me in the shoulder. "Really? Why would you share that with everyone?"

"I didn't think it was a secret." I looked at Marcia and Finn, who were staring at each other. Marcia was glaring, obviously blaming him for bringing along his douchebag friend. "Sorry, I assumed we were all friends here, and I thought you were talking to Marcia about it this morning."

"You weren't so good that the first thing I did was go and tell my best friend about you." She stared at me. "You're such a jerk. Why would—you know what? Forget about it. I thought you were different, but I guess not."

"You thought I was different to what?" I shrugged. "I don't know what that means."

"Just nothing. Shall we go get breakfast?" She turned to Marcia and Finn, and they both nodded.

We headed toward the table and sat down, and I started to feel a little bit annoyed with myself. Of course I'd known she wouldn't want me to share what had happened, but I hadn't been able to stop myself. It was like I wanted to ruin our friendship, even though I liked her. I didn't understand.

"But I mean, my tongue was good, right? Would you say the best you've—"

"Come on now, Brody." Finn's eyes narrowed. "That's enough."

Marcia shook her head. "You're so immature."

"You're telling me," Susie said. "I thought we had a connection yesterday. I thought when you were telling me about your brothers that—"

"Brothers?" Finn interjected and looked confused. "What are you talking about?"

"Last night, Brody was telling me a story about his brothers and a three-way duel they had."

Finn looked at me in confusion. "I've known you since college, and I clearly remember you only having one brother. Right?"

"I need to make a call," I said, pushing back my chair.

I could feel my muscles tightening as I jumped up and headed out of the room. I looked back and saw that they were all staring at each other in confusion.

I forgot. I'd gotten so relaxed and comfortable with Susie that I'd forgotten, and now everything was going to come out. People were going to ask questions and demand answers to things. I didn't want to talk about that. I never wanted to talk about it. Why? Because I'd been a jerk. Because I told them that I'd gone down on Susie. This was my punishment.

I walked to the lobby of the hotel and looked at my phone for a few seconds. I just needed to get out of here. As fate would have it, my phone started ringing, and I picked up.

"This is Brody. What's up?"

"Hey, Brody. It's me, Marianna."

"Who?" I said, not recognizing the voice or the name.

"Marianna from LA? I'm a cheerleader for the Lakers."

"Um, okay."

"I was just wondering if you were going to be in town this weekend because we're having a party."

"No, I... Actually, you know what? Sure. Where's the party?"

"It's in Beverly Hills. It's going to be so cool. I knew you'd be down. You know, I've been thinking." Her voice lowered.

"Thinking about what?" I said.

"I've been thinking about *Mr. Brody*."

"Oh, yeah?" I grinned.

"Yeah." She laughed. "And that thing you got me to do that I said I would never do."

"I'm not recalling," I said, oblivious.

"You know. Back door." She giggled.

"Um, okay." I didn't want to tell her that I'd fucked around with so many women that it was hard for me to remember one from the other. Though, it was weird, because I could still remember the way Susie had tasted, and I could still picture her face when she'd orgasmed, and the way her brown eyes had—

I had to stop it.

"I'll fly in tonight," I said. "This is your number?"

"Yeah, of course. Isn't it saved in your phone?"

"Yeah, it is," I lied. "I'll call you when I get into town. Maybe we can hook up tonight and party or something."

"Sounds good," she said, and with that, I hung up.

I was meant to fly back to New York with Finn and Marcia and Susie, but I needed to get away from them. I needed time to think. I needed to just be me, and I couldn't do that if I was surrounded by them. I couldn't do that when a part of me wanted to be a better man. The truth was, that there was no part of me that could ever be a better man than I was now.

I'd ruined my chances of love and happy ever after a long, long time ago.

SEVENTEEN
SUSIE

"So what was that all about?" I stared at Finn, my face twisting tight.

"I have absolutely no idea." He shook his head. "I just asked him a question."

"Why is he so sensitive?" Marcia said. She sighed. "And he's really rude. I can't believe he said that about last night." She reached over and touched my hand. "You okay, Susie?"

"I'm fine. I mean, he's a pig. I knew he was a pig, and I should've remembered that before I allowed myself to get close to him. I thought he was a better guy than that, but I guess I was wrong. He's just a jackass. He's like all those other jocks I knew in high school and college. All he cares about is getting some."

"You didn't sleep with him, did you?" Marcia asked, a nervous expression on her face.

"No." I chewed on my lower lip. I wanted to add more, but I didn't want to say anything in front of Finn. He was Marcia's boyfriend, but I didn't know him like that. I certainly didn't want to talk about my sex life in front of him.

Finn cleared his throat and looked at Marcia. "I don't think she wants to talk to me about that."

"Very perceptive." I laughed. "Oh, what is Brody's problem? And where did he go?"

"Just let him be. He'll be fine." Finn shrugged. "We're flying out today, so I'll have a talk with him when we get to the airport."

"Okay." I nodded. "But I had a question for you."

"Yeah, what is it, Susie?" He shook his head and smiled at me warmly. "Sorry, I didn't mean to sound annoyed, I'm just frustrated with Brody. You okay?'

"Yeah." I nodded. "And I understand. I was just thinking, you said that he only has one brother, and he told me he has two brothers. I'm confused."

"You and me both," he said.

"He was lying to one of you, obviously. But why?" Marcia said. "It doesn't make sense."

"I know," I said. "And, it was very clear to me that he has two brothers because he told me he's the middle child."

Finn looked like he was concentrating really hard. "What are you talking about a younger brother? He only has an older brother. I met him once."

"Oh, have you met any of his other family members?"

"No. Just his older brother once in college. He didn't really talk about his family much. I guess he wasn't close to them. I mean, a lot of people aren't."

"Huh," I said. "And you're sure he never mentioned a younger brother? Or that the younger brother came to visit?"

"Well, I certainly would've remembered if he did." He scratched his head for a couple of seconds. "I'm trying to think of when his older brother came and if he said if another brother stayed home. No, I clearly remember him telling me he only had an older brother, and that he wished he had a sister at times because maybe then he'd understand women a bit more. I remember because we were sitting in a strip club, and a lady had just thrown a drink in his face and..." He paused as Marcia glared at him. "Oops, sorry."

"It's fine," she said. "Now I know you and Brody like to go to strip clubs."

"He is a man, Marcia. Plus, I'm sure he's not going now. Are you?"

"I mean, no?" Finn said with an impish grin, and then he started laughing as Marcia poked him in the arm. "Of course not. Why would I care about looking at other women's naked breasts when I have your naked breasts to look at?"

"Sometimes you're just as bad as Brody."

"Hey, now. That's not fair," he said. He then cleared his throat. "Okay, Brody's coming back to the table." I looked toward the entrance as Brody started walking back toward us with a huge grin on his face. I frowned as I realized he looked jovial and happy, completely opposite of his demeanor when he'd left the table. What was going on? Was he bipolar or something? Was he a manic depressive? Was he Dr. Jekyll and Mr. Hyde? I didn't understand.

"Hey, sorry about that," he said as he sat back down at the table. "By the way, I'm not going to be coming back to New York with you."

"What?" I said, staring at him. "What do you mean?"

"I'm going to actually catch a flight to LA." He grinned. "You know who just called me?" He looked at Finn.

"No, no idea."

"Marianna." He winked.

Finn shook his head. "Who?"

"Remember those Lakers cheerleaders we hung out

with that weekend in Vegas?" Brody wiggles his eyebrows. "You know, back-door Marianna."

"No," Finn said, glaring at him. "I have no idea what you're talking about."

"Her best friend was the one that let you titty fuck her in the back of the limo."

"What the fuck, Brody?" Finn looked pissed off. I could see Marcia's face crumpling, and she looked like she wanted to cry, which I completely understood.

"What the fuck is your problem?" I looked over at him. "Why are you trying to get Finn into trouble as well?"

"What? He couldn't remember who I was talking about, so I figured I'd let him know exactly what went down that weekend so he could remember. How many times do you see your best friend titty fucking a cheerleader in the back of a limo?"

"Brody, we need to talk." Finn jumped up and walked over to his friend. "I've had fucking enough of you this weekend."

Brody held his hands up. "What?"

"What's your problem, dude? What is this about?"

"What do you mean?" Brody said. "I'm just telling you guys I'm not going to be making it back to New York with you, and you don't have to deal with me being such an asshole."

He looked at me then, and even though he had a bravado to his voice, I could see pain in his eyes, which I didn't quite understand. He looked like a young boy. And for a few seconds, I just wanted to hold him close to me and ask him what was wrong. But I was too upset to want to comfort him.

"Come on, dude. Let's talk." Finn stood there.

"I'm hungry."

"We'll come back in a second, okay?"

"Fine," Brody said and nodded, and he followed Finn out of the restaurant.

"What the hell was that about?" Marcia leaned across the table, rolling her eyes.

"I don't know, but are you okay?"

"I'm fine," she said and sighed. "I knew Finn had a past. He's gorgeous and a billionaire. It's not like he was a virgin when we met."

"Of course, you're still upset, though."

"Yeah, I'm upset. Who wants to hear about their boyfriend titty fucking a cheerleader in the back of a limo? And you know Brody said that just to upset me. He was probably hoping I'd be pissed off at Finn so that he wasn't the only one that was in time-out.

"I just don't understand him, Marcia. Yesterday, we had such good talk. He told me a story about his brothers, and he was massaging me, and..." I sighed. "I just don't get it. I thought we were developing a real connection. I'm not crazy. I didn't think he was falling in love with me, and I didn't think he was going to ask me to be his girlfriend or anything like that, but I thought we would be solid friends, and maybe friends with benefits."

"Friends with benefits? Really?" Marcia stared at me. "You know you can't do friends with benefits."

"I know that normally I can't do friends with benefits, but I've never met a guy like Brody before."

"And what's so special about him? You yourself said he's a douchebag."

"Yeah, but he's a troubled douchebag." I laughed. "You know how it is. We're always drawn to the men with issues. I don't know if it's the maternal instinct in us, but we want to fix them and make them whole again."

"And you want to fix Brody?"

"No, I don't want to fix Brody. But I want to be able to understand him."

"And once you understand him, then you want to fix him?"

"I'd be lying if I said I don't want to know what the root of the problem is. And yeah, if I knew, maybe I'd be able to help him. Obviously there's something wrong."

"Oh my gosh. Sometimes guys are just assholes, Susie. Sometimes there's no deeper issue. Sometimes they just want to fuck around. And I think Brody Wainwright is that sort of guy."

"I don't think so," I said. "I know I sound like I'm totally in la-la land, because he's been totally rude to us, but I think there's something else. I do think that underneath it all, he's a good guy."

"And that's why you dropped your panties for him?"

"Girl, I didn't have on any panties to drop." I winked at her, and she started giggling.

"Okay, I know we both hate him right now, but a girl's got to know. Was he good?"

"What do you mean was he good?"

"With his tongue. You know what I'm talking about."

"Let's just say that his tongue gave me the best orgasm I've ever had in my life. The best."

"Wow." She looked impressed. "Really?"

"Yeah." I sighed. "I mean, I'm curious to know what he can do with his cock now."

"Oh my God, Susie."

"What? I'm being honest."

"So are you going to sleep with him?"

"I may have considered it before, but now that he's going to LA to hang out with a cheerleader and not even coming back to New York, I honestly don't ever want to see him again."

"But you know he's Finn's best friend, so you're probably going to see him again."

"If I see him, I'll just be like, 'Hello, goodbye.' That's it."

"What do you think is going on with his family life?"

"Huh? What are you talking about?"

"The brothers."

"Oh, yeah. Sorry. I was thinking about something else. I know something is really weird, because I know he has a younger brother. He wouldn't have talked about his family and siblings that way if he didn't. And the fact that Finn is so sure that he only has an older one means there's some reason why he's not talking about it. Do you think they fell out?"

"Oh my God, I got it. I know what it is."

"What is it?"

"He probably slept with the younger brother's sister."

"What?"

"Oops, sorry. I'm talking too fast. He probably slept with the younger brother's girlfriend or fiancée or wife, and the younger brother cut him off or something. Said, 'You're dead to me. Never speak to me again. Pretend I don't exist.' And that's what he's doing."

"You think so?" I said. "I know he's a jerk, but I don't think he would hook up with his brother's girlfriend. Has he made a move on you at all?"

"No. He knows not to. Finn would kill him."

"Yeah, but I'm sure his brother would've killed him too. And you would think that he'd have more allegiance to his brother than to a friend."

"True." She nodded. "Honestly, he hasn't even given me a flirtatious look." She licked her lips. "I've never once felt uncomfortable around him, you know? He hasn't tried anything with me."

"And you're gorgeous, so if he was going to be a dick, he would do it with someone like you."

"Maybe," she said. "But then, what is it? Why would he lie?"

"Maybe he's not lying," I said. "Maybe... Oh, I don't know. It's confusing. But obviously, that upset him and hurt—"

"You know what?" Marcia interrupted me.

"What?"

"Maybe that's why he's going to LA."

"What do you mean? To meet his brother?"

"No, no, no. Maybe the conversation triggered something in him, and the only way he's dealing with it is being an asshole." I nodded slowly.

That made sense because pretty much every time he'd been an asshole had been when he hadn't liked the way a conversation had gone. I looked at her thoughtfully.

"But you know what?" I continued. "I'm not his savior. He needs to figure that shit out on his own. I've got my own heart to protect."

EIGHTEEN

BRODY

"So you're really going to LA?" Finn looked at me with a disappointed stare. I could tell from the look in his eyes that he was annoyed, and I didn't blame him. But, frankly, I'd just about had enough of everything.

"Yep. I'm going to LA."

"Dude. Why would you say that? In front of Marcia and Susie? Are you trying to make me look like a jerk, just like you?"

"How am I trying to make you look like a jerk, Finn? You were there with me. Am I lying?"

"Dude. You do not tell a guy, in front of his girlfriend, to remember the time he was motorboating some chick in the back of a limo."

"So you do remember?"

"How could I forget that night? It was crazy." He shook his head. "But those days are behind me. How do you not understand that?"

"I was just trying to remind you who Marianna was because you couldn't seem to remember."

"Does it really matter? If you want to go to LA, go to

LA, but don't treat me like shit in the process. Don't treat my girlfriend like shit. And you sure as hell better not treat her best friend like shit. What's come over you, dude?"

"It's not my fault if Susie thinks that we have something just because I went down on her once. Like, that's nothing. We haven't even fucked."

"Brody, do you listen to yourself? Do you hear what you're saying? You're the one that's being a jackass here, not Susie."

"I just don't want her to get the wrong impression because we had some fun last night. She seems like she might be clingy, just like Marcia."

"Whoa, hold up. Are you trying to dis my girlfriend now?"

"Let's be real, dude. You got some sex and now—"

"Hey." He grabbed me by the collar, his other fist clenched at his side. "Don't make me break your arm. You've got an awfully expensive contract to play out."

"Okay, okay. My bad," I sighed. "It's just been a rough couple of days."

"I thought you had fun."

"It was cool, but it's just been a lot."

"What's the deal with you having two brothers and only telling me about one of them?"

"Dude, I don't know why you're making it into something it's not. Does it really matter? It's not like I have sisters you can bang."

"Why do you talk about women like that? Why do you—"

"I'm sorry. It's my bad. I'll apologize to Susie. I'll apologize to Marcia. I'll make it all good. Okay? And then I got to get to the airport, because my flight is in a couple of hours."

"So you're not even going with us to the airport?" He looked even more disappointed. "Brody, man."

"What, Finn? Just because you're coupled up and domestically blissed doesn't mean I have to be as well. I'm living my life. I'm doing the things you wish you could be doing."

"No, man. I don't wish I could be screwing nameless women."

"Well, then that's on you." I looked at my watch. "Anyway, I need to go pack. I want to eat my breakfast and then go."

"Brody." Finn sighed. "Look, we've been friends for a long time, and I know we're dudes and all, and we don't show our feelings. I've never really asked you much about your past or your childhood or anything, but if there's ever anything you need to talk to me about, let me know. And if you don't want to talk to me," he said quickly, "I know a good therapist."

"I don't do therapy." I narrowed my eyes. "I'm not fucking crazy."

"I didn't say you were crazy. But if you've got shit in your past that you don't really want to talk about with anyone? Maybe a therapist could help. Get some of that anger out, or whatever's causing you to be such an asshole."

"She's really got your nutsack tied up. Huh?"

He shook his head. "I still have faith in you, but it's really, really low right now."

"Okay, I'm so sad. Like whatever, dude. I've got millions of dollars and hundreds of girls that will be there for me."

"Do you think they'll really be there for you? Would they be there for you if you didn't have any money?" He stared at me for a few seconds, and I just stared back at him.

"Well, that's a question I don't really have to ask right

now because I have millions." I shrugged. "And to be honest, my portfolio is looking better every day. So I'm not really worried about—"

"That's not the point."

"Anyway, let's go finish breakfast."

"You and I, we need to have a longer talk when we get back to New York." Finn sounded aggravated, and my guilt doubled.

"Okay," I said. "Whatever."

"Whatever, indeed." He shook his head, and we headed back toward the restaurant.

Marcia and Susie gave us a quick glance and then turned back to face each other. My heart was racing. And even though I wouldn't admit it to Finn, I was ashamed of myself. What I'd said wasn't cool—telling them about Susie and my previous night. And then telling Marcia about Finn motorboating someone else... I knew that wasn't cool.

When they brought up my brothers, well, it struck a nerve in me, because I didn't normally talk about my younger brother. In fact, I made it a point never to mention him, because I didn't want people asking me questions. I didn't want to think about those days.

Ever since I'd gone to college, I'd created a new identity. And yet when I'd been talking to Susie and telling her stories, I'd forgotten about those guards. I'd told her stories that I'd never told anyone else. I told her things that I hadn't even wanted to remember until the words had come out of my mouth.

"Hey," I said as I stopped next to the table. I cleared my throat and ran my hands through my hair, then spoke first to Marcia. "I'm sorry about what I said earlier. It really wasn't my place to talk about Finn and his previous life. I hope I didn't upset you."

"It's okay," Marcia said with a brief nod. She didn't smile, and I could tell she didn't particularly like me in this moment. I'd have to work on earning her forgiveness, because she was Finn's girlfriend, and I was pretty confident they'd get married one day. There was no way I was going to lose my best friend because I was a douche to his girlfriend.

I then looked at Susie who was obstinately ignoring me. I sat down in the chair next to her and tapped her on the shoulder. "Can we speak?" I said.

She turned to me slowly and stared at me with blank eyes. "What?" She was pissed. And I deserved it, of course, but it didn't make me feel good.

"Hey, I'm sorry as well. I shouldn't have told them about last night, and I've been acting very immature."

"Yep. You have been."

"I'm just sorry, okay? I had a really good time with you, and these last couple of days have been special. I didn't mean to ruin that by being a jerk, and I really hope I didn't ruin our friendship"—I made a face—"or more."

"There is no more, Brody." She rolled her eyes. "Are you joking?"

"Well, I don't know. Last night was fun and maybe one day we'll sleep together."

I couldn't stop myself, and she just stared at me with huge eyes.

"Brody Wainwright, I wouldn't sleep with you if you were the last man on earth. Do you understand me? Not if you were the last man on earth."

"Wow. Okay. Well, tell me how you really feel."

She sighed, and I could see that Marcia was looking pissed off as well.

I held my hands up in the air. "My bad. I'm sorry. I

guess I have a teenage boy sense of humor when I'm among women. I should really clean up my act."

"Yeah, you should," Marcia said pointedly. Then she looked at Finn. "I really hope you're not like this as well, Finn."

"Hey, you know me," Finn replied. "Don't shoot the messenger."

"What messenger are you?" Marcia said. "What message are you giving us?"

"Maybe I used the wrong phrase there. But don't shoot me just because he's my friend. He knows he messed up, and he's sorry. Right, Brody?"

"I'm sorry. I'm really sorry. And"—I sighed—"I'll make sure when I see you guys again, I'll mind my Ps and Qs. Okay?"

"Whatever," Susie said, and Marcia just nodded.

I looked at Finn and he shrugged.

"Well, I think I'm going to have an omelet," I said to no one in particular.

Marcia and Susie started talking about something that had nothing to do with the situation, and I just sat there, uneasy. I'd really fucked up. I'd taken a good situation and made it bad. And yet I didn't know how to fix it. I didn't know how to be sincere. And I didn't know how to tell Susie that the last few days had been some of the best days of my life. That talking to her and getting to know her had been really, really special.

I didn't know how to tell her, because I didn't even want to admit it to myself. If I analyzed what I was feeling too much, I had a feeling my walls would come down, and there was no way I was going to open up my heart to any more pain. I'd been through the most heartbreaking pain of my life, and I barely made it through. I couldn't afford to let my walls down and make myself vulnerable. Again.

I sat there for a couple more minutes, being ignored, and realized that I couldn't sit there anymore. I jumped up and bowed. "I'm going to go pack and catch a cab to the airport. Catch you later, guys."

I walked away from the table before any of them could respond and let myself into the hotel room. I packed up my stuff quickly and sat on the bed for a couple of seconds, staring at Susie's side of the mattress. I bent down and sniffed the pillow for a few seconds. It was creepy, but it smelled like her. I sat up, wondering what the hell I was doing with my life. Wondering if I would ever feel complete and whole again.

I grabbed my suitcase and headed toward the door, and it opened just as I was about to walk out. Susie walked in, a bleakness in her brown eyes as she stared at me.

"So you're going now," she said softly. I nodded. She opened the door wider. "You can go, then." She ushered to the empty space.

"Close the door," I said. My heart was racing fast, and I almost felt like I was made of glass about to shatter into a million pieces. I didn't understand how or why I was feeling this way. "You finish your breakfast already?" I asked.

"No. But I didn't want you to leave without me saying goodbye." She licked her lip nervously, and my heart expanded at her words. She truly was a good person—too good of a person for me, almost certainly. But that didn't stop me from wanting her, needing her.

I like you, I wanted to say. *I really like you.*

But the words didn't come.

"I don't know what's going on with you, Brody. I don't know why you've been such an asshole, and why you always have your defenses up. But I just wanted to say that I had a good time getting to know you these last couple of days. The real you. The you behind the mask. And I like that guy. He's a nice guy, a fun guy. And I do believe that he's real." Her voice caught.

She rubbed her forehead and played with her hair, and I wanted to pull her toward me and kiss her.

"I know I probably sound like a fool," she said, "because you haven't really given me any reason to say any of these things. But I hope you know that you are worthy of so much more than you're allowing yourself to experience."

"I don't know what you're talking about," I said.

"You do." She nodded and looked into my eyes, and we just stared at each other for what felt like an eternity.

I could drown in her eyes. I could live forever in their silky expanse. She was beautiful—probably the most beautiful woman I'd ever seen in my life. She had an aura to her that was loving and caring and kind, and it made me feel comfortable. It made me feel safe, which was a weird feeling for me. I couldn't explain it. I didn't know what to think, or what to say.

"I hope you have a nice flight to Los Angeles," she said. "I hope you have a good time with your cheerleader friends and whoever." Her voice cracked and she looked away.

I wanted to tell her that I didn't want to go, but I had to. I had to be the Brody Wainwright that I was comfortable being. I had to be the man that didn't get close.

I grabbed her hands and pulled her toward me, and I bent down and kissed her hard. I pulled on her curls, and she arched her back so that her breasts were crushed against me. She kissed me back passionately—her hands around my neck, digging into my skin. I grabbed her around the waist and thrust her into me so that she could feel the hardness of my erection against her. I wanted her so badly. I needed her. My hands moved up her waist and cupped her breast, and she whimpered against my lips.

And then she pushed me back, anger in her eyes. "Don't kiss me," she said. "You don't get to do that."

"You seem to like it," I said softly.

"Maybe," she said. "But just because I liked it doesn't mean I want to do it with you. Just because I liked it doesn't mean you're a good guy. Go, Brody. Go do whatever you want to do. I've had enough of you."

NINETEEN

SUSIE

"I'm so sorry, Susie." Marcia squeezed my hand as we sat on the plane. "He's such a jerk-off."

"I know, but what are you going to do?" I sighed. "He is who he is. I mean, he doesn't owe me anything. It's not like he's my boyfriend. It's not like he's my man. We had a couple of kisses and some fun, and I can't lie, I wouldn't take it back."

"You wouldn't?" Marcia looked surprised.

"No, I wouldn't. I know you think I probably would, right?"

"Girl, you were going off on him literally just two seconds ago."

"Yeah, because he sucks. But I had a good time, and it reminded me what it is to be a woman. It reminded me that I want love and sex and all those things."

I heard Finn groaning in the seat next to Marcia. "Do you girls really need to have this conversation right now?" He chuckled. "I was kind of hoping to not talk about Brody."

"Yeah, well, he's your friend, and you're the one that brought him. We didn't even want to go camping, so..."

"So, what? You didn't have a good time camping?" Finn asked.

"It was fine," Marcia said. "What did you think, Susie?"

"It was fun. Honestly, I wasn't sure that I'd like it. I prefer to be pampered, but I had a good time. Would I go every weekend? Probably not. Would I go again? Yeah, sure. It was cool. Maybe not with Brody but..." I wrinkled my nose. "Anyway, let's talk about something else. I don't want to give him the time of day."

"Good thinking, Susie." Marcia nodded. "Shall we watch a movie?"

"Yeah. And actually, I think we have Wi-Fi on the flight."

"Yeah. So?" Marcia looked confused.

"Let's message Shantal and Lilian. Maybe they want to grab a drink when we get back to the city."

"Oh, yeah. That will be really fun. Maybe we can go dancing."

"Excuse me?" Finn cleared his throat. "When are you guys expecting to do all this?"

"I was hoping tonight," I said seriously. "I need a good dance, and I need—"

"Hold up a second. Marcia," Finn said.

"Yes, Finn?" she asked him softly.

"You're going to go out tonight?"

"Well, if Shantal and Lilian are down."

"But what about me?"

She laughed. "What about you?"

"I was hoping we could spend the evening together."

"Really? You want to spend more time with me? I thought you'd be fed up with me by now."

"Fed up of you?" he said. "I haven't even come close."

I rolled my eyes. "This is sickening. I'm all for a good love story, but really, this is past Hallmark now. This is... I don't even know. Maybe Harlequin romance sort of romance."

"Don't be jealous," Marcia said with a small, sincere smile. "Anyway, Finn, after we go dancing, I'll come out to your place, okay?"

"Promise?"

"Yeah, of course. I want to spend the night with you as much as you want to spend the night with me."

"Oh my gosh, guys. Really?"

"What?" Marcia said. "Now, text Shantal and Lilian and see if they even want to go out tonight, or this whole conversation was moot."

"Okay." I grabbed my phone and connected it to the flight's Wi-Fi. "I guess this is one perk of flying first class."

"You can say that again." Marcia giggled. "I could get used to this."

"Me too." I sighed. "Only problem is, I don't have a rich boyfriend who can afford to fly me first class, and I don't even have money to fly it myself."

"I know," Marcia said. "I don't know what I'll ever do if Finn and I..." She paused and looked at him.

He raised an eyebrow. "If you and I what?"

"Nothing," she said.

"You're not thinking about us breaking up, are you?"

"No, of course not. Why? Are you thinking about breaking up with me?" She started giggling. "Don't you know I'm only with you for your money."

He shook his head and chuckled. "You're lucky I know that's not who you are."

"That's why I'm able to laugh with you about it." She

grinned at him and I could see the love pouring out of both of them. They really got each other.

"You're going to be the woman I marry. You're going to be the mother of my children. So no."

I stared at them for a few seconds and smiled. Even though I was jealous, and even though they made me want to puke, and even though they made me want to poke my own eye out with a fork, I still loved their banter and camaraderie. They were perfect for each other. And frankly, it surprised me to see that Finn could be such a romantic. He'd never struck me as someone that would be sappy with his words, but he totally was. He totally loved Marcia.

I thought about Brody and wondered what it would be like to have a relationship like that with him. I almost burst out laughing at the thought. There was no way Brody could ever be romantic like Finn. He just didn't have it in him. It wasn't part of his DNA. And for a few seconds, that made me like him more.

It was crazy, but I missed him. I hated him and he made me want to scream, but I missed him. I missed the touch of his lips. I missed the way his eyes followed me around the room. I missed the way he touched me lightly when he wanted my attention. And I missed the way he listened. He had said I was a good listener, but he was a really good listener as well.

I sighed deeply as I realized I was thinking about him too much. I couldn't afford to think about him. I couldn't afford to think of him as a good guy. I didn't want to get my feelings hurt.

I opened my text messaging app and sent a group text to Lilian, Shantal, and Marcia.

Susie: Hey, girls. What's up? Marcia and I are back this evening. Want to go out dancing?

Shantal: Hey! I'm down.

Lilian: I'm down too. Can't wait. Where should we go?

I looked over at Marcia and grinned. "Shantal and Lilian must've really missed us. They both already responded, and they want to go dancing too. They just want to know where we're going."

"Oh, wow. Awesome." Susie smiled. "I don't know. Is there anywhere you want to go?"

"I'm not sure. Let me ask Shantal. She always seems to know the good places.

Susie: So I don't know where we're going to go, but Shantal, do you have any ideas? I want to get drunk. I want to dance and flirt with as many cute boys as possible.

Shantal responded immediately.

Shantal: I know the place. So how was camping?

Susie: It was fun... I have something to tell you guys, though.

Lilian: Oh my gosh. What? What, what, what? Tell me.

I responded quickly.

Susie: It will be easier to tell you in person, but let's just say it involves a boy.

Shantal: What boy?

Susie: Brody Wainwright.

Lilian: No fucking way. Not the baseball player.

Susie: Yep. And trust me, you don't want to know what happened.

Shantal: Oh my God, you fucked him and you didn't use protection. Are you pregnant? :P

Susie: No, I didn't have sex with him, and no, I'm not

pregnant. But thank you very much for asking. Also I wouldn't know if I was pregnant already.

Shantal: I was seeing some high child support!

Susie: You're horrible.

Shantal: I know.

I looked over at Marcia and started laughing. "Shantal is absolutely crazy. She asked me if I was pregnant and then said I could have gotten some major child support."

Finn groaned. "Not Shantal from the office."

Marcia looked at him. "Honey, pretend you didn't hear this conversation. I don't want you mentioning it to her at work."

Finn shook his head. "You know what? I think I'm going to watch a movie. I'll see you guys when we land."

"Well, you see us right now as well." I grinned. "We're not leaving the plane, unless there are parachutes I don't know about."

He laughed. "Very funny, Susie. You know what I mean."

"I know. Enjoy your movie." I watched as he slipped his earphones in and selected a movie on the screen, and then I turned to Marcia. "He's a nice guy. I'm really happy for you."

"Thank you. He's definitely one in a million." She smiled happily. "And for what it's worth, I am really sorry about Brody."

"It's okay," I said. "He seems like he's got issues. And while that's not my problem, I can't blame him for being who he is. He never promised me anything. He never lied to me. And yeah, maybe he's a bit immature, and maybe he opened his mouth when he shouldn't have, but who am I to judge? I've done the same thing in other situations, I guess."

"You're such a good person Susie," Marcia said, looking at me with love. "I'm so glad you're my best friend."

"I'm so glad you're my best friend, too, Marcia. I love you."

"Love you too. And we're going to find you a great man soon."

TWENTY

BRODY

There were a gaggle of women surrounding me. The music was loud and obnoxious, and the stares of almost everyone in the room were on me. Even though I was in LA, a city full of rich and beautiful people, I still stood out. Single and good-looking, I was someone that men and women alike envied and wanted.

Marianna stood about ten yards away from me, her hands wrapped around a blonde's waist as they made out. She kept peeking glances at me to see if I was watching, and I nodded every so often, but frankly, I didn't care. I didn't find it to be a turn on whatsoever.

I sipped on my rum and Coke and looked at my watch. I was ready to go home, but I had detoured my trip to come to LA. I couldn't let it be for nothing.

"Hey, Brody." Marianna walked up to me, holding the hand of the blonde she'd been snogging.

"What's up?"

"I'm so glad you made it to LA. I wish you were pitching for the Dodgers, though."

"Nah, the Dodgers suck. Nothing like the Yankees." I

grinned.

"Or the White Sox," the blonde said from behind her.

"They're okay," I replied. "I prefer the Cubs."

"Oh, you're so funny, Brody." Marianna said.

I stared at her. In her see-through outfit, I could see every part of her body, from her nipples to her cleanly shaved pussy. Nothing was a mystery. I wondered why she was wearing clothes at all.

"So Heather and I were wondering..."

"Who's Heather?" I asked nonchalantly.

"I'm Heather," the blonde said, staring at me with wide blue eyes. "I met you like ten minutes ago."

She had a little bit of an attitude, and I wanted to tell her that she looked like all the other plastic blondes with fake boobs at the party, but I kept my mouth shut.

"Anyway, Brody. We were wondering if you wanted to go back to my place," Marianna said with a smile. "I was thinking that I'd love to feel you in every hole."

And then she put her index finger in her mouth and started sucking.

"In every hole?" I said, staring at her.

"Yeah. How hot would that be to know that I had Brody Wainwright filling me everywhere I could be filled."

"That'd be fucking hot," the blonde said. She walked over to me and put her hands on my shoulder before bringing her lips in close to mine.

"And then you can do me after you do Marianna," she said with a wink. "And maybe if you're lucky, you can watch us do each other."

I blinked and looked at her and then looked at Marianna. I just didn't care. None of this was turning me on. I wasn't hard or even close to being hard.

I jumped up. "I've got to go to the restroom," I said quickly.

"We'll be waiting for you, big boy," the blonde said, and then Marianna laughed.

"I want to meet Mr. Brody again."

I wanted to groan at her term for my cock. He wasn't Mr. Brody, and he wasn't interested in being with her again. I navigated around the room until I found the restroom. I opened the door and saw two guys snorting cocaine.

"Hey, Wainwright. What's up?" a tall guy asked me, a huge grin on his face.

"Not much. What's up, dude?"

"Nothing. You want some coke?"

"No, thanks."

"We got some E as well. What's your poison?"

"I'm clean. Thanks." I turned around and exited the room and saw a staircase. I decided to go up the stairs and see if I could find a private bathroom there. I was in some mansion in Beverly Hills that belonged to some music producer I'd never met before. I'm sure he wouldn't care. I walked up the stairs and saw that many other people at the party had had the same idea.

To the right, there was a couple having doggy-style sex. The girl was screaming and crying out while the guy pulled on her hair. They didn't seem to care who was watching. As I passed by, the guy lifted his hand to get a high five from me, and I shook my head.

I couldn't believe this was the sort of party I had liked to go to before. And even worse, I couldn't believe I didn't like it now. What the fuck had come over me?

I found the master bedroom, and while there was a couple on the bed making out, there appeared to be no one in the bathroom. I opened the door and locked it behind me, then took a deep breath. I turned on the faucet and splashed my face with cold water. What the fuck was going on?

I unzipped my pants and pulled out my cock, closing my eyes and trying to picture Marianna and her blonde friend making out. Her nipples. Her pussy.

But I couldn't get myself hard.

"Fuck it." I banged my wrist against the wall and cried out. "Fuck it, fuck it, fuck it."

I didn't understand what was going on. I quickly put my cock back into my pants, zipped up, and pulled out my phone. I had about five missed texts and two missed calls from Finn, as well as a bunch of calls from different women. I called Finn back, and he answered immediately.

"Yo, Brody. What's up?"

"Just returning your million calls. What's up, pops?"

"I just wanted to make sure you were okay." He cleared his throat. "You okay?"

"Yeah, I'm fine. I'm here in the 90210 partying it up with a bunch of bitches."

"Okay. And you're enjoying yourself?"

"Fuck yeah. I just got offered to have a threesome with a hot blonde and a hot brunette. Tonight is going to be—"

"Brody," Finn cut me off. "If you were having that much fun, you wouldn't be calling me back."

"Dude, I just took a restroom break."

"Uh-huh. What's going on?"

"Nothing. I'm just here partying it up. What's up with you? Banged your mistress for the night, and now she's fallen asleep?"

"I'm going to ignore that. And no, Marcia went out."

"Wow, okay."

"Yeah, her and Susie went out with some of their friends. They've gone dancing."

"They what?" I froze. This was not what I'd expected to hear. "What do you mean they've gone dancing? Dancing where?"

"I don't know. Some club."

"And you just let them go by themselves?"

"What do you mean? They're with each other."

"Dude, any guy can hit on them. They're hot. Do you really want—"

"I trust Marcia. She wouldn't do anything."

"But what about fucking Susie?" I said, almost shouting.

"What about her? The last thing I heard, she was free and single. If she wants to hook up with a hottie, she can."

"What the fuck are you talking about? Hook up with a hottie? Who's she hooking up with?"

"Whoa, Brody. Calm down. Dude, what the fuck is going on? I thought you got some blonde bouncing on your dick tonight. What do you care about Susie?"

"What's her phone number?"

"Dude, I'm not giving you her number."

"Please, Finn."

"Marcia will fucking kill me."

"Please."

"Why would I give you her number when you're about to get laid by some fucking blonde chick? Has she already bounced on your cock?"

"No. I'm not fucking tonight, okay?"

"Has she sucked your cock?"

"No."

"Has she given you a hand job?"

"No."

"Have you sucked on her titty?"

"What the fuck, Finn?"

"Look, dude. I'm not going to give you her number unless I know you're legit here."

"What do you mean I'm legit? Give me her fucking number, Finn."

"If you're going to talk to me like that and give me an attitude—"

"Please. LA's not happening for me. I'm going to come home tomorrow. I'd like to talk to Susie. I'd like to apologize properly."

"She's done with you. You know that, right?"

"Well, maybe that's because I fucked up. But I can fix this."

"You did. And honestly, Brody, she'll probably hook up with someone tonight because she thinks you're hooking up with someone."

"Why the hell would she think I'm hooking up with someone?"

"Because you told all of us that you were going to LA to meet up with some cheerleader that you fucking banged in the back of a limo the last time you saw."

"I never said I did that."

"Dude, it was implied."

"How was it implied?"

"Well, when you kind of mentioned that I was motorboating her friend, it was implied that you were doing more than me because you're a dirty dog."

"Oh, what, and you're just a dog?"

"I'm not a dog anymore, dude."

"Fine. That's why I need her number, okay. I need to talk to her."

"You like her, don't you?" Finn started laughing and I groaned.

"What the fuck are you talking about?"

"I mean, you like her, like her."

"No, I don't. I just want to make sure she's okay."

"I'm not giving you her number unless I get something from you."

"Like what?"

"Do you like Susie?"

I hesitated. "Okay, she's cute."

"She's cute? What does that mean?"

"She's fucking gorgeous. Yeah, I want to bang her."

"Brody."

"Okay, it's about more than banging. Look, if I wanted to bang her, I could've banged her already. I'm the one that stopped it from happening."

"And you stopped it because..."

"I don't fucking know. Because she's your girlfriend's best friend?"

"That's not why you stopped it, dude."

"Okay, I stopped it because she deserves more than a fucking quick bang in a cheap hotel room."

"The hotel room wasn't that cheap, Brody."

"You know what I mean, Finn."

"So you like her."

"Yeah, maybe I do. Maybe that's the reason I can't fucking get it up tonight, even though two horny-as-hell women were all over me, fucking telling me—actually, pretty much begging me—to fuck them all night long. So yeah, something is wrong with me."

"And that is?"

"Okay, you're right. It's fucking Susie Benedict. She's in my head. I can't stop thinking about her. I want to talk to her."

"We're finally getting somewhere."

"You're an asshole, Finn?"

"I aim to please."

"So you're going to? You'll give me her number?"

"Yeah, but hold on. I'm going to have to go into my database at work. I don't just have it saved in my phone, you know."

"Hurry the fuck up. I want to speak to her."

"Calm your horses."

"If she fucks someone tonight..."

"Then what, Brody? What are you going to do? She can do whatever she wants."

"I know, but..." I sighed. "Never mind. She can do what she wants, you're right."

"Okay, I got her number. You ready?"

"Yes."

"Here you go." He rattled off the numbers and I wrote them down quickly, my heart was racing like I'd just been given a gold crown or something.

"Great. Thanks."

"So Brody..."

"I've got to go, dude," I said and hung up. I punched Susie's number into my phone and dialed quickly before I could stop myself. It rang and rang while I was getting angrier and angrier.

I thought it was about to go to voicemail when a breathless girl picked up. "Hi. Who is this?"

"Susie, is that you?"

"Yeah, it's Susie. Who's this?"

"It's me."

"Who's me?"

"Brody."

"Oh," she said softly. "How the hell did you get my number?"

"Where are you?"

"I asked you a question."

"And I asked you a question too. Where are you?"

"I asked my question first, Brody."

"Where the fuck are you?"

"I'm at a club with Marcia, Shantal, and Lilian. Why?"

"You're not at some guy's place?"

"No. Why would you think I'm at some guy's place?"

"I don't know. I wasn't sure if you had your mouth full of dick before you picked up my call." Jealousy seared through me and I knew that she had every right to tell me to fuck off. I was treading in deep waters and all my emotions were threatening to drown me.

"What the actual fuck?" She cleared her throat. "I don't know whether to laugh or cry, but you're totally inappropriate, Brody."

"I'm sorry." I sighed and took a deep breath. "Please ignore that. I'm trying to put my best foot forward here. That just came out."

"Where the fuck are you? Do you have your tongue up some girl's pussy?"

"No. The only girl's pussy I want to be fucking right now is yours."

"Brody," she said, her voice cracking slightly. "What the—"

"I fucked up, Susie. I know that. I'm sorry."

"I don't know what to say, Brody. Where are you?"

"I'm in LA. I'm in a bathroom in a house in Beverly Hills. Actually, you can't even call it a house. It's a mansion."

"Okay."

"And look, I just realized something."

"What did you realize?"

"So Marianna, the girl I came to see, was with her

friend. They were making out and touching on each other's boobs, and they came up to me and told me that they wanted me to fuck them senseless. And you know what?"

"No. What, Brody?"

"I didn't even get fucking hard. And you know why?"

"Why, Brody?"

"Because you're the only one I want to be with right now. You're the only one I want to fuck. I couldn't even fucking jack off thinking about them."

"Do you think this makes me feel better? Why do you think I care that you can't fucking get hard for two bimbos, and that you tried to jack off thinking about them? What the fuck? Am I meant to be happy? Am I meant to be excited? Do you think this is a compliment?"

"So what, you're not interested?"

"Am I interested in what, Brody? Fucking you? Because you can't get hard for two fucking sluts?"

"Yeah. That's exactly what I'm trying to say," I said, even though that was totally not what I wanted to say.

"You're an idiot, and I'm going now." And with that, she hung up.

"Fuck it." I banged my fist against the wall. I royally screwed that up. I was a fucking idiot.

I took a deep breath and called her number again. I'd get it right this time. I'd say, "Susie, I like you. I've never experienced this before, and all my words are coming out wrong, and I'm sorry. Can I take you to dinner tomorrow night?" That's what I'd say.

But she didn't pick up. The phone kept ringing and ringing and ringing.

I sent her a text message.

Brody: Please, Susie, I need to talk to you. I'm sorry. Please call me back?

I hit send and waited five minutes, but no text came back in response. I called her number again, but it kept ringing.

"Pick up the fucking phone, Susie," I grunted into her voicemail and then hung up. "Shit."

I called back, contrite. "I'm sorry. I shouldn't have said that. Please call me back."

And then when I called back again, it went straight to voicemail. She was ignoring me now. I didn't know if she'd blocked my number or just turned her phone off, but I was pretty much done for the night.

I splashed my face with cold water again and realized I was probably the biggest idiot and asshole that the world had ever seen. And maybe Finn was right. Maybe it was time for me to see a therapist.

It had been suggested to me in high school, but I was a Wainwright. We didn't have problems. We didn't have issues that needed to be dealt with by seeing a therapist. But maybe I did need to speak to someone. Maybe I did need to figure out how to face the demons of my past.

I slowly opened the door and stepped into the bedroom. The couple that had been making out were now fucking. The girl was on top, riding him, and she grinned at me as I walked through the bedroom.

"Don't look," she said, shaking her breasts, and I just chuckled and left the room.

I walked down the stairs and looked at the crowded party. It was weird. Just a couple of weeks ago, this would've felt like one of the best parties I'd ever been to. But now, it was meaningless. It was nothing.

I watched as Marianna walked up to me, the blonde nowhere in sight. She stopped next to me and tried to kiss me. I averted her lips, and she looked pissed.

"What the fuck, Brody?"

"Sorry. I've got to go."

"What do you mean you've got to go? What about us and tonight?" She placed her hand on the front of my pants and squeezed. My cock gave her nothing in response. I grabbed her hand and pushed it away from me.

"Sorry. Tonight's not a good night for me."

"But I have all these plans for us."

"I'm sorry, Marianna. It's just not—"

"I let you fucking take my anal cherry, punk. You're going to turn me down now?"

"I very much don't believe I took your anal cherry." I stared at her and shook my head. "Not trying to be rude, but it seemed like you had kind of done it before."

"You jackass." She glared at me. "How dare you talk to me like I'm some sort of hoe!"

I pressed my lips together and took a deep breath. "Marianna, I'm sorry if I led you to believe that something was going to be happening tonight, and I'm sorry if I offended you the last time we had sex."

"How would you fucking offend me? I've fucked hotter guys than you. I've fucked richer guys than you. Shit, I've fucked guys who were more famous than you. I fucked guys who are better at fucking than you. So fuck off, Brody Wainwright."

Then she slapped me across the face and walked away. I stared after her, rubbing my cheek, and sighed. I'd deserved it. I'd always been an asshole to women, and I'm sure there were many more out there who wanted to slap me.

I headed out of the front door and looked at my phone. There were no missed calls, no missed text messages. I tried Susie's number once again, and it went immediately to voicemail.

"Hey. I'm really hoping that we can meet and chat. I've come to a lot of realizations recently. And while I know it doesn't really mean anything to you, it would mean a lot to me just to talk to you. And even if nothing else comes of it, I'd very much like to be friends."

I hung up and then called an Uber. It was time to go home.

TWENTY-ONE

SUSIE

"I can't believe Brody just called me," I stared at Shantal, Lilian, and Marcia. They all looked at me with different expressions, though none of them looked surprised. "Why do none of you guys look surprised?"

"I had a feeling he'd call you. He just seems like that sort of guy."

"What do you mean?"

"The sort of guy that desperately wants what he can't have," she said with a shrug.

"Yeah." Lilian nodded. "He's a total playboy. I have a friend that knew someone that hooked up with him in LA. Let's just say he has a voracious appetite, and I'm not talking about food."

"Oh, wow," Shantal said.

"I mean, I can't lie," Lilian continued. "If he wanted to fuck me, I would've said yes. He's gorgeous, girl. Absolutely gorgeous. I can't believe you turned him down."

"I know, but he knows he's gorgeous," I said. "He's just so cocky, and I'm not looking to hook up with a guy that doesn't care about me. I know that sounds totally unrealistic in this day and age, especially if it's a one-night stand or something, but is it too much to ask to want the guy to kind of like you?"

"Not at all," Lilian said. "You deserve the best."

"Yes, you do," Marcia said. "We all deserve the best."

"Well, you've got the best," Shantal told Marcia. "I still think it's crazy that you're dating our boss, but I'm not going to say anything."

"Please don't," Marcia said. "It's not like I *tried* to date the boss. It's just that he and I ended up working out."

"Lucky bitch," Lilian said, and we all laughed.

"Okay. Don't look now," Shantal said, "but I think there's a guy checking you out, Susie."

"What do you mean? What guy?"

"I said don't look! There's a blonde guy. Oh my gosh, he's coming. Okay, everyone stay cool."

I couldn't stop myself, and I looked over my right shoulder. There was a gorgeous guy heading toward me with long blonde curly hair and big blue eyes. He slightly resembled the actor Travis Van Winkle.

My heart was pounding. In the back of my mind, I was thinking about Brody and his calls, but what had he expected me to do? What had he expected me to say? It wasn't my fault he wasn't having fun at the party. How dare he tell me that there were two women that wanted to fuck him. Was he trying to make me jealous?

"Hi." The tall blonde guy stopped in front of me.

"Hi," I said.

"What's your name, sexy?"

"Susie," I said with a slight smile. This guy was pretty confident. "What's your name?"

"Bradley."

"Oh, well, it's nice to meet you, Bradley."

"You too." He looked around at my friends and smiled. "Nice to meet all of you, actually. I don't mean to be rude, but I just had my eye on this curly haired vixen."

"Well, thanks." I laughed, playing with my curls.

"I was wondering if I could buy you a drink," he said softly.

I looked at my friends, not sure what to do.

"Go on," Marcia urged me. "Go have a drink. We'll be right here."

"Okay." I looked back at Bradley and nodded. "A drink sounds nice."

"Awesome. It must be my lucky night," he said as we headed over to the bar. "I hope you don't think I'm too forward. I don't normally do stuff like this."

"Really?" I said, surprised. "You seem pretty confident."

"I guess maybe it was the whiskey I had earlier tonight." He shrugged. "But when I saw you standing there, I just knew I had to say hello."

"Oh. Well, I guess that's pretty cool."

I didn't really know what to say. He was a very handsome man, and he had a sweet smile and genuine eyes, but I wasn't interested in him that way. My mind was full of Brody—wanting to talk to him and wanting to know exactly what he was doing. I turned off my phone because he'd kept calling and texting me, and I just wasn't ready to have a conversation, and certainly not while I was out with my friends. How rude would that have been?

"So what are you thinking about?" he said softly.

"Sorry, what?" I blinked, realizing I'd completely spaced out.

"I was just asking what you were thinking about. You seemed to be in another galaxy." He ran his hand through his hair and reached over and touched my lips. I blinked and he grinned. "Sorry. You just have the most beautiful lips."

"Oh, thank you," I said, taken aback.

"I want to kiss them."

"Oh." I stared at him with wide eyes. This was getting dirty pretty fast.

"I know I said I'm not forward, but I like to be honest, you know?"

"Sure," I said as we stood next to the bar.

"What d'you want to drink?"

"I guess I'll get a tequila sunrise."

"Knew it," he said, almost shouting.

"Sorry, knew what?"

"I knew you'd be the sort of girl that would want a cocktail. No beer for you."

"Okay. Yeah. I don't really like beer."

"Yep. I knew it."

"Well, good for you. You're smart, Bradley."

"Handsome and smart," he said.

"Yeah. So what are you going to get to drink?" I looked over at my group of friends, who were staring at me, and tried not to make a face. I should have known it was too good to be true.

"Probably another whiskey. I mean, it got me to you. So maybe it will prove to be lucky again tonight."

"What do you mean by that?"

"I don't know," he said. His eyes roamed down my body, all the way to my feet. "Wow. Nice heels."

"Oh, thank you."

"Are they Louboutins?"

"No. I don't have money for Louboutins."

"Maybe I'll buy you a pair one day."

"Okay. That would be cool," I said, not really knowing

what to say. It's not like I wanted him to buy me heels. I didn't even know the man.

"But I'll only buy them on one condition."

"What condition is that?"

"If you walk over me with them."

"If I what?" I said.

"If you walk over my body in your high heels," he almost purred. "And then slip them off and give them to me."

Okay. Oh God. What's going on? I wanted to scream and shout and run away from him. "Then I want you to walk over me with your bare feet."

"Okay."

"Then I want you to sit on my face."

My jaw dropped then. "Sorry, what?"

"I want you to sit on my face. But before I eat you out, I want to suck on your toes."

"I think we've had some miscommunication here. I don't think we're looking for the—"

"As soon as I saw you in those heels, I knew you were the one for me. You look like the sort of woman that can take charge, walk all over me, and whip me."

"I don't think I'm interested in whipping you."

"But what if I gave you a little pleasure and pain?"

"Not interested thanks."

"You didn't read *Fifty Shades of Grey*?"

"I didn't, no. Why?"

"Oh, because doesn't every woman want a Christian Grey?"

"No, I don't think so, but maybe you should join a kink site to find a woman that does."

"So you're telling me you're not into whips and chains?"

"Yeah, I'm telling you that."

"You don't like it when a man sucks on your toes?"

"I can honestly say I've never had a man suck on my toes. Bradley, while it's been very nice getting to know you, I think I'm actually going to have to go back to my friends without the tequila sunrise."

"What the fuck? I already ordered it."

"No, you didn't. No one's taken your order yet."

"Yeah, but I was about to order. I mean, when I saw you," he mumbled. He was getting flustered and red. "So what? Now you think I'm some jerk just because I told you I like to suck on toes?"

"No. I mean, good for you. I just don't think my toes are the ones you're going to be sucking on."

"You're too good for me to suck on your toes?"

"You know what? I'm going to walk away from this right now. It was very nice meeting you."

"Whatever, bitch," he said and walked away.

I stared after him for a few seconds and then walked over to my friends.

"What the hell happened?" Marcia said, looking at me with wide eyes. "It looked like it got heated, and then he just walked away."

"Girl, this is not my day. Let's just say, dude had a foot fetish and didn't seem happy by the fact that I wasn't interested in him sucking my toes after or before—I don't even know—me whipping him."

"Whipping him?" Shantal said. "Say what?"

"Don't even ask."

Lilian shook head. "Oh my gosh, what is up with the men in this fucking city?"

"Girl, the question should be *What is up with all the men in the world,* period?"

TWENTY-TWO

BRODY

"Alex, I really appreciate this," I said to my manager over the phone. "I know it's not customary for you to send the private jet unless we're on work business, but I really need to get back to New York as soon as possible."

"No worry, Brody. You're one of our star players. I didn't even know you were going to be in LA."

"Yeah, it was sort of a last-minute thing, and I shouldn't have come."

"So you'll be back in New York in a couple of hours, then?"

"Well, I don't know that the pilot will fly that fast. But I'll be back tonight, or rather tomorrow morning. I appreciate it."

"No worries. I'll see you on the field. Rodriguez said he can get back on the field."

"That's awesome."

"Yeah, it's great news. We're going to have a press conference next Thursday. Do you think you'll be able to make it?"

"If you need me, you know I'll be there, Alex. I owe you one."

"Great. Thanks, Brody. And hey."

"Yeah?"

"Don't do anything I wouldn't do on that plane."

"What do you mean?"

"You bringing some chicks back with you?"

"No. Trust me, no." I chuckled, though I didn't think it was funny.

"I'm surprised. Aren't you the lady magnet?"

"I don't know about that. But hey, thanks anyway, Alex."

"Sounds good. I'll chat to you later."

"Bye." I hung up the phone and stared at the private airport in Burbank. I was thankful that my manager had been able to secure one of the private jets for me to fly me back to New York City. This way, I didn't have to wait for a commercial flight to take me in the morning.

I needed to see Susie. I needed to talk to her, and I was hoping that she'd let me take her to breakfast in the morning. I wasn't sure how I was going to make that happen, but maybe Finn would give me her address. It was a long shot, because she might have hooked up with someone else.

I sighed and tried not to think about what I would do and how I would feel if I found out she'd been with another man. It wasn't like she owed me anything, and Finn was right. For all she knew, I was hooking up with someone else as well. Just because I'd called her late at night didn't mean anything. It didn't stop anything. And I knew that no matter what she'd done, if she'd been with another man or whatever, I didn't care, because it wasn't for me to judge her. While I was jealous as all get out, I knew it wasn't my place to be judgemental.

"Hey, are you Brody Wainwright?"

As, the pilot headed toward me in the seating area, I jumped up.

"Yep. That's me."

"We're flying into New York?"

"Yeah, if possible. I'm not sure if you can get a spot or if we have to go to Newark."

"It'll be easier if we go to Newark, but we might be able to get a spot at JFK. I'll call air control and see."

"Okay, awesome."

"I can let you know, and you can let your driver or."

"It's fine," I said. "I'll get an Uber or a cab or something."

"Whatever works for you."

"I appreciate you coming out this late to fly me back."

"No worries, Mr. Wainwright. We work for the New York Yankees." He grinned. "Let's play some ball, eh?"

"Yeah, let's play some ball." It was weird how everyone looked at me and thought of me as this awesome pitcher and baseball player, but I had never really been interested in baseball until college. Until I had decided to carry on the legacy that had been cut short in my family.

I wasn't the one that was meant to carry on the baseball legacy. I wasn't one that had grown up throwing around the ball with my dad and being the envy of every other player on the school team. I wasn't the one that teachers said scouts would be after. I was just me, nerdy Brody.

I took a deep breath and ran my hand through my hair. I was still trying to reconcile how I could have gone from my true self to my inauthentic self. Because even though I loved baseball, and even though I was thrilled at every game I won, it wasn't the same. It wasn't as satisfying. It wasn't as motivating to get up every morning.

When I'd been in school, I'd wanted to find a cure for cancer. I'd wanted to research molecular DNA and more specifically recombinant DNA. But all of that had been cut short. I wasn't even sure if Finn knew how much I'd loved science, how much I kept up with the latest technology and breakthroughs.

"We're ready to go now, Mr. Wainwright." The pilot signaled to me, and I followed him toward the gate. There were two air stewardesses standing there beaming at me.

"Good evening, Mr. Wainwright," they chorused.

"Welcome aboard," the redhead said. "Let us know if you'd like something to drink or anything else."

"I'm good for now. Maybe some water?"

"Okay."

I smiled at them both. I knew what else was on offer if I was interested. It was always on offer for me from everyone. Well, except from Susie. But the fact that I didn't even care showed me how much I'd changed. Other women meant nothing to me now.

They went about closing up the cabin, and my phone started beeping. I wasn't going to check it, because I was nervous it was Marianna begging me to come back and let me fuck her. And I knew if I picked up and spoke to her, I'd tell her just how off-putting her desperation really was. For some reason, I did check my phone, and my jaw dropped when I saw it was Susie.

I answered quickly. "Hey."

"Hey," she said. "What are you up to?"

"Not much. You?"

"Oh, not much either. I saw you left a couple of messages."

"Yeah, just a couple." I chuckled. "I'm surprised you're calling me back. It's late there, right?"

"Yeah, but I just got home, and it's weird being alone. I wanted someone to talk to and figured, well, you had called me, so maybe I could call you back. I didn't want to be rude. But if you're busy with your women or..."

"No, I'm not busy. What about you? Did you meet any hot guys?"

"Well, there was one."

"Oh yeah?" I said, jealousy searing through me.

"Yeah. He told me he wanted to buy me a pair of shoes."

"Oh, really?"

Yeah, Louboutins. And they're like $1,500 a pair."

"And what did you say to him?"

"I said no, thank you." And then she started laughing a loud, beautiful sound that was infectious.

I started laughing as well, even though I didn't know what she was laughing about.

"Why are you laughing?" she said.

"Because you are, and I can't stop myself. Why are you laughing?"

"Because the guy had a foot fetish, and he was a complete and utter creep. And, well, it just reminded me how sucky the guys in New York are."

"Oh, so you're saying I'm not the only one?"

"No, you're not the only one, Brody."

"Well, I don't know if that makes me feel better or not."

"It should make you feel better," she said. "It made me feel like you weren't as bad as I initially thought."

"I just haven't told you about my foot fetish yet."

"Please don't tell me that," she said with a giggle.

"If I did, would that be a problem?"

"Yes," she said. "Definitely yes."

"You sound pretty adamant about that."

"I am very adamant about that, so I'm letting you know now."

"Don't worry. I don't have one. So where are you?" I said, lowering my voice.

"What do you mean where am I? I told you I'm at home."

"I know you're at home, but where at home are you?"

"Oh my gosh, Brody. You're not trying to seduce me, are you?"

"How am I trying to seduce you?"

"You know what I mean. Are you trying to have phone sex?"

"I mean, if you were willing." I started laughing before she could respond. "But I'm not exactly in the right place for that."

"Oh," she said. "I didn't realize you were still out."

"Yeah, I'm kind of partying with women."

"Sorry. It's none of my business."

"Would you care if I was partying with women?"

"Yeah, I guess."

"Well, I'm not. At least not now. I was earlier. I was at a party and they were offering the goods, and I wasn't interested."

"Okay, so where are you now?"

"I don't know if you'd believe me if I told you."

"Try me," she said.

"I'll tell you where I am if you answer one question for me."

"Oh gosh, here we go."

"No, it's nothing sexual. I promise." I smiled. All of a sudden, I was feeling happier than I'd felt in a long time.

"Fine. What's the question?"

"Why did you call me?"

"I told you why. You called me and left messages."

"We both know you didn't want to talk to me earlier." I laughed. "And for good reason. I've been a jerk and an asshole. But…"

"But what?" she said.

"What made you change your mind?"

"Honestly?"

"Yeah, honestly."

"I guess I kind of got used to talking to you every night before I fell asleep. I know it sounds corny."

"No, it sounds sweet," I said, my heart racing.

She sighed. "I kind of miss you too. Is that weird?"

"Why would it be weird?"

"Because we don't really know each other, and we don't really like each other."

"Speak for yourself, Susie. I like you."

"You know what I mean. We're just not in the same place in our lives."

"Maybe that's true, but that doesn't mean we can't miss each other, right?"

"I guess. So where are you?"

"I'm on a plane."

"You're what?"

"I'm on a plane."

"Where are you going now?"

"I'm coming back home."

"To New York?"

"Yep."

"But you just got to LA."

"And I realized I made a bad choice," I said softly. "I should've come back to New York with you guys."

"Oh. What made you leave right away? I didn't even know they had flights right now."

"They don't, but I'm on a private plane. I should get in early in the morning. And actually..."

"Yeah?"

"I was hoping that perhaps I could take you to breakfast."

"What?" She sounded shocked, and I wasn't sure if that was a good or a bad thing.

"I want to see you, Susie, and I want to take you to breakfast."

"I don't know, Brody."

"You called me for a reason, right?"

"I mean, yeah."

"You missed me and I missed you. Well, let's grab breakfast tomorrow and see."

"See what?"

"I don't know. We'll just see."

"I'll meet you for breakfast on one condition," she said.

"What's the condition?"

"You'll tell me why you got upset today."

I froze for what felt like an eternity but could only have been about thirty seconds. Telling her why meant telling her things I'd never shared with anyone else. But in my heart, I knew that if there was anyone I was going to share it with, she was the one I would want to tell.

"Okay," I said. "We can talk about it."

"Really?" She sounded shocked.

"Why do you sound surprised?"

"I guess I just didn't expect you to be okay with that."

"Surprisingly, I am. But yeah, breakfast tomorrow? I think I have to turn off my phone. We're about to take off."

"Okay," she said. "Where shall we meet?"

"Text me your address. I want to pick you up."

"Oh, you don't have to do that. We live in New York."

"No, I'm going to come to your place. Text me your address, okay? And I'll be there at 10:00 a.m."

"Sounds good."

"Sweet dreams, Susie."

"Thanks, Brody. Have a good night."

"Dream of me," I said. "And if you want..."

"Yeah?" she said.

"You can masturbate to me as well."

I started laughing as she hung up, feeling like I was floating on air.

I thought about her request to hear more about my brothers. It was going to be hard, and I didn't know that I was ready to go there yet, but for someone like Susie, for someone that was willing to give me a second chance, I knew I had to step it up. I knew I had to give her a reason to actually want to give me a second chance. I didn't know what I wanted or what she wanted or what any of it meant, but I just knew I had to give it a chance. Both for me and for her.

Susie: Brody is coming to take me to breakfast. Am I making a mistake?

Shantal: Holy shit! No way!

Lilian: You took the words right out of my mouth.

Susie: Close your mouths, girls. I called him when I got back from the club.

Lilian: Why?

Susie: Because shoe fetish guy made me realize that all men are dogs. I mean, no one is perfect. And sometimes, in life we have to see what we can and can't accept.

Marcia: Not all men! And omg, what the hell is going on, Susie? Did you hit your head or something?

Susie: No, but Brody and I had a good time in California. Aside from all the crazy shit.

Marcia: And him telling the entire restaurant that you'd had oral sex the night before.

Susie: He wasn't that loud.

Marcia: He certainly wasn't quiet.

Shantal: That's what she said.

Susie: Hahaha. And I know he was an idiot, but I figure going to breakfast won't hurt.

Shantal: Oh boy, you like him.

Lilian: You want his D in your P <------P

Susie: What is that meant to be?

Lilian: Oops, I meant O<-----------P

Shantal: Shouldn't it be V<--------------P

Marcia: Or just plain P<-----------------P

Susie: You guys are so stupid.

Lilian: Am I lying or am I telling the truth?

Susie: I'm not going to sleep with him at breakfast. :P

Marcia: Uh huh. Btw, don't think Finn and I didn't hear you guys making out in the tents... We totally knew you guys were hitting it off.

Susie: No shame in my game. He's hot.

Lilian: He's also a cocky bastard though. Did he or did he not go to LA to bang some cheerleader??

Shantal: Dude is a walking STD.

Susie: He didn't hook up with anyone. In fact, he actually regrets going to LA.

Marcia: Is that what he said?

Lilian: Sounds like the cheerleader had a loose vajajay and now he wants what Susie's cooking. JK, btw, I'm sure the cheerleader is wonderful. She sounds like me in a past life...like three months ago.

Shantal: He want's a piece of Miss Susie. Ooh lalala. I need me a man.

Lilian: Me too! Preferably one with a big dick.

Shantal: What's big to you?

Lilian: Anything over 6 inches.

Marcia: Really, girls? This chat is for us to tell Susie to get rid of Brody.

Shantal: Not until she sees if he can shake the motion in her ocean.

Lilian: No, if he can bake the shake in her chicken.

Shantal: If he can cream the scream in her bed.

Lilian: If he can eat the meat that she shares.

Susie: What the hell?

Shantal: Sorry, I'm still hungover from last night.

Lilian: Wanna grab brunch?

Shantal: I'm in! Susie? Marcia?

Marcia: Sorry. Finn is taking me to Philly today to try out some restaurant he loves.

Susie: And you already know I'm going to be meeting Brody.

Shantal: Tell us everything when you get back home.

Susie: Okay.

Marcia: Make him pay for it! Give him hell.

Susie: I will. :)

I LAUGHED as I put my phone down and grabbed my hair-spray. I looked at the mirror and smiled at my reflection. I looked so different with my hair straight, and I wondered if Brody would notice. I also wondered if he'd act like a jerk again. I had no idea what to expect when he showed up. He was the sort of guy that kept me on my toes; that was for sure. I knew the girls thought I was making a mistake. I knew they thought I should just ignore him and move on with my life, but the truth of the matter was that I wanted to see him. I wanted to talk to him. I wanted to touch him. And I wanted him to kiss me again. I wanted to feel his hands sliding up my waist to my breasts. I wanted to feel him against me.

I sighed as I closed my eyes. I needed to get out of the sensual frame of mind. Yes, I was excited to see Brody, but I was still very upset at him. I didn't want him to think I'd forgiven him just because I'd agreed to go to breakfast.

I wanted to see if he would be the kind of man that fairy tales were made of. If he had a deeper side, a sensitive side. I wanted to see if he was the man that I thought he was inside.

I reapplied my lipstick and looked at my phone. He'd texted me when he landed, and I only had fifteen minutes until he arrived. I was far too excited to see him. I almost felt like I was going on a first date. And even better, I was finally going to get to know him better. I was finally going to see the man he was inside.

TWENTY-FOUR
BRODY

"Sunshine is my best friend." I sang a made-up song as I made my way down the street. "No rain today. It's a beautiful day."

There was something about New York; the buzz of people was palpable. It made me feel alive. I decided to cut through the park on my way to see Susie. I spotted a man with a cart selling roses and I ran over to him.

"I'd like three roses, please."

"Which colors?"

"Well, what do the colors symbolize?" I wanted the flowers to mean something to Susie. I wanted her to know that I was putting thought and care into our meeting. She wasn't just getting simple red roses from me.

"Red for love, purple for passion, light pink for congrats, orange for fascination, white for new love, cream for charm, and yellow for friendship." He pointed at each rose. "So which ones do you want?"

"I'll take a white one, a yellow one, and a purple one, please." I grinned. "I'll be unique."

"That's thirty dollars."

"Wow, okay." I reached for my wallet and pulled out some cash. As I was waiting for my change, two young boys came running toward me.

"Hey, there. Are you Brody Wainwright?" asked the older of the two boys as he stopped next to me. He tugged on my jeans, and I nodded as I smiled down at him.

"Yeah, I am."

"Our dad says you're the best pitcher in the entire MLB."

"Well, I wouldn't say that." I shook my head modestly. "Perhaps one of them."

"You are the best. Oh my gosh. I can't believe we're meeting you. Can you believe that Patrick?" The boy spoke to who I assumed was his younger brother, who looked up at me with big blue eyes. I froze for a second as I stared down at him. The name Patrick always did that to me.

"Hi," the boy said. "Can I get your autograph please?"

"Of course." I nodded. "Do you have a pen and paper?"

"No." He stared at me with big, wide eyes, and I looked over at the flower man.

"Don't suppose I could borrow a piece of paper and a pen?"

"That'll be five dollars," he said.

"For paper and a pen? I'm going to give you the pen back."

"Yeah, but paper is expensive these days. You know what the pandemic has done to—"

"Fine. Fine. Just add it to my bill."

"All right then, Mr. Wainwright," he said with a wink.

"Okay, so you're Patrick. And what's your name?" I asked the older boy.

"Michael."

I stilled as I stared at them. There was just no way.

Michael and Patrick? The names of my older brother and my younger brother.

"Okay. So should I write one to both of you or individually?"

"I'd like my own, please," Patrick said. And I nodded.

I wrote "Patrick, keep on pitching. Brody Wainwright." And then I wrote the same thing to Michael. I handed them the papers and turned toward the flower guy.

"Here's your pen. Can I have the flowers?"

"You got the flowers, sir. They're in your hand."

"Oh yeah. Thanks. Well, it was good seeing you both," I said to the boys.

I walked away quickly, my brain frazzled. What were the chances of meeting two young boys by the names of Michael and Patrick? It wasn't as if those names were unique, but still.

And then I looked back, and Patrick was throwing a ball to Michael, and they were staring at me. They probably would've wanted me to play with them. Kids loved it when you threw them a ball, something they'd be able to talk about for pretty much the rest of their lives. But I just couldn't.

I rubbed my forehead and looked to the sky. The blues suddenly seemed gray and my mood was changing. I didn't want to sing. In my gloom, I had a flashback to when I was a child, and my brothers Patrick and Michael had been playing with a ball.

"Hey, go further, Michael." Patrick had shouted. "Further, further."

"It's too far," Michael had said. "You can't throw that far."

"I can. I'm going to be the best pitcher in the world. I have the quickest fastball in all the land," Patrick had said as

he'd thrown the ball to Michael. Michael had chased after it as it fell to the ground.

"Yeah, you can throw far, but you're not that fast."

"I am too," Patrick had said. "I'm going to be a professional baseball player, and everyone is going to come and see me."

My memory drifted off. I'd been sitting on the grass about fifty yards from them, a book in my hand. I think it'd been about Tom Sawyer or Huckleberry Finn by Mark Twain. I'd loved reading in those days and much preferred to be with a book than to be playing sports. My brothers used to make fun of me. But they'd learned over time that nothing was going to change.

I was the odd one out. The ugly duckling. The black sheep of the family, so to speak.

And then another day, when we'd all gone blackberry hunting. After we'd picked and eaten as many blackberries as we could, they'd wanted to go swimming in the creek. I'd wanted to go home, because I was tired and hungry. I also wasn't much of a swimmer. They'd teased and provoked me, said I wasn't their real brother if I didn't go with them.

And so we'd gone, and it'd actually been fun. And that had been one of the only times in my life where I'd actually felt like I belonged, that I was actually a Wainwright. That Michael, Brody, and Patrick were The Three Musketeers and not just two brothers and their third, the odd man out.

I blinked as a fly flew into my eye, and I walked over to a bench and sat down. I was discombobulated. I stared at the roses in my hand and placed them on the bench next to me.

"Patrick," I said, looking back at the little boy who was now gone. Not sure where to, but it seemed fitting. "Patrick, where are you?" I stared up at the sky. "Are you there? Are you watching me? Do you think it's ironic that I'm a baseball player now? Or do you hate me? Do you hate me for living your dream? For being better than any of us ever would've thought possible?"

I was getting choked up. I wanted to cry. I picked up my phone and decided to call my brother—the one that was still available to answer my calls. The phone rang five times, and then he picked it up.

"Hey. What's up, dude?"

"Michael, it's me. It's Brody.

"I know. Long time no speak. You don't call a brother back."

"Sorry. I've been busy."

"I know I read about it in the papers. You're a Yankee now."

"Yeah, I guess I am."

"Thought you would have gone to Philly, personally. But who cares what I thought."

"You didn't put money on it, did you?" Though I already knew the answer to that. He'd definitely put money on it.

"Sure did. Felt like a fool when I lost my thousand dollars, and my friends also weren't happy when they lost money too. I mean, how does the brother of one of the top baseball players in the country not know who he's going to play for?"

"I didn't know. And I didn't know you bet on it. So."

"Yeah, yeah. It's not your problem. It never is."

"Hey, now. I didn't call to argue."

"I'm just surprised you called, to be honest."

"I know. I haven't been in much contact lately."

"Yeah. Mom and Dad said they haven't heard from you in a while."

"I'm going to call them soon, but..."

"But what, Brody? They've already lost one son. Now they feel like they've lost another."

"I do my best."

"Sending them money doesn't make up for the fact that they never hear from you."

"It's just... You know, Michael. You know why it's hard."

"They didn't mean what they said. They were grieving. It was a bad time for all of us."

"I know, but I can't help but think they wish it had been me instead of him."

Michael sighed. "You can't think that hasn't crossed everyone's mind, Brody. It is what it is."

"I blame myself. I..."

"Let's not talk about it, Brody. Okay? It's no one's fault."

"Do you ever think about him?" I said.

"Of course. Every day. He was my best friend."

I knew when he said that he didn't mean to hurt me or exclude me. It was just a simple truth. Even though he and I were closer in age, he and Patrick had been together every moment of the day. It had almost been like they were twins.

"But anyway. How are you, Brody? I see you in the papers a lot. Looks like you're getting a lot of tail. Ironic, huh?"

"Yeah, I guess so. How are you and Nancy?"

"She's fine. Pregnant again, of course. Three boys, two girls, and another one coming. I just don't know how I'm supposed to—"

"I can send you money. I can help out."

"I don't want your goddamn money, Brody. And anyway, it doesn't matter. I think we've only got a few years left."

"What are you talking about? What do you mean a few years left?"

"I'm in love with someone else, Brody."

"What?"

"Remember Brittany?"

"Brittany? Brittany from high school?"

"Yeah. Well, she's back in town, and she's taken a liking to me again, and let's just say she misses the good ol' days."

"You're not cheating on your wife. Please tell me you're not cheating on Nancy. She has been there for you—"

"She has no time for me, Brody. She's always with the kids. She doesn't even shower half of the time. She stinks. Of course I can't tell her that because then I'd be a bad husband, but she's really let herself go. She must have gained like fifty, sixty pounds."

"Hey, Michael. You sound like an absolute douchebag right now."

"What? You're my brother, right? And didn't you say we should always tell each other the truth?"

"Yeah, but that's not cool, dude."

"Who are you to talk? I see you with models every fucking week online. I'd love some pussy from an actress or a model or, shit, any woman that hasn't let herself go."

"You know what, maybe this wasn't the right time for me to call you, Michael."

"Yeah, maybe not. Maybe you can send me some tickets to make up for it."

I sighed. "I'll put them in the mail." And then I hung up.

I sat there for a few seconds, not knowing what to do, but knowing that I felt like absolute shit. Suddenly I realized that I was supposed to be at Susie's place to take her for breakfast and tell her about my sordid past.

But in that moment, that was the absolute last thing I wanted to do.

I hated myself and I hated my family. I wouldn't tell anyone that out loud because I felt ashamed. But what had happened all those years ago had ruined everything. It had absolutely ruined everything. And I felt desperately sad for myself, for Michael, for my parents, for Nancy, and for Michael's kids. Everything was shit.

I knew I couldn't see Susie. All I needed right now was a drink. Just to forget. Just to feel numb again. I knew I'd be disappointing her, but maybe it was for the best. Maybe I really wasn't ready. Maybe I was meant to be alone. I didn't deserve happiness after everything that had happened. I had been given the world and yet none of it meant anything.

I wasn't happy, and there was nothing I could do to change it. There wasn't a time machine. I couldn't go back in the past. I was screwed, and I wasn't going to bring another person into my fucked-up life. I wasn't going to bring another person into my inner turmoil. Susie deserved better than that. She deserved a good man. And that wasn't me.

Disappointment coursed through me as I sat on the couch. It was 9:00 p.m., and Brody hadn't shown. Not only had he not shown, he hadn't even texted or called. And when I texted him, there was no response.

The doorbell rang, and I got up and walked over. Marcia stood there, along with Shantal

Lilian and Shantal. Shantal was holding up a bottle of wine in her hand.

"Hey, girls. Come in," I said as I ushered them into the apartment.

"You okay?" Marcia asked, looking at me with a worried expression.

"I'm fine. You could've used your key, you know. You could've just come in."

"I didn't want to intrude."

"You live here."

"I know, but I'm barely over here anymore, and I'm sure you just don't expect me to come in."

"It's fine, Marcia. Your name's on the lease as well."

"I know." She grinned. "You okay?"

"I'm okay." I nodded. "Let me go and get some wine-glasses and a wine opener." I headed to the small kitchen and grabbed our supplies before heading back to them. I handed it over to Lilian, who gave it to Shantal, who opened the bottle of wine. She generously poured the red liquid into glasses, and I took two deep gulps.

"Did you hear anything from him?" Lilian said.

"Nothing. I don't know if he's playing some sort of game or what."

"You sure he's okay?" Lilian asked. "You think he would've texted that something came up or something."

"I think he was paying me back. He was calling me Saturday night, trying to talk, and I turned off my phone. And now he did the same thing to me."

"That's so immature, though," Marcia said. "Why would he do that?"

"Come on now, Marcia. The one thing we know about Brody is that he's immature."

"True, but—"

"But nothing. It doesn't matter anyway. Obviously, he's letting me know exactly what he thinks about me and our friendship, and he just doesn't care."

"That sucks. I'm so sorry," Shantal said. "Why do guys have to be such dickheads?"

"I wish I knew," I said.

"I could call Finn and ask if he's heard from him," Marcia told me, and I shook my head.

"No, I don't want to get Finn involved. Plus, I don't want him to get upset at Brody and then cause drama. It is what it is, right? I don't care."

"You do care, though, Susie."

"It's fine. Yeah, I thought he could possibly be a nice guy. I thought that there could be something there. Yeah, I liked him. I liked talking to him. I think he was handsome, but obviously it means nothing. He didn't show up, so whatever. Let's talk about something else."

"I don't suppose you want to go dancing again?" Shantal asked, and I shook my head.

"No, I really don't think I'd be up for that."

"Makes sense," Lilian said. "So guess what I did." She held up her tote bag.

"I don't know. What did you do?" I didn't really care, but I had to pretend.

She pulled out four rectangular envelopes. "We're going to do face masks."

I laughed. "Okay."

"And"—she pulled out a box—"this is a board game."

"Like, what, Monopoly?"

"No, it's called Lords of Waterdeep."

"Lords of who?" I stared at her, confused.

"It's kind of a riff on Dungeons & Dragons."

Marcia's eyes widened. "Say what? We're not teenage boys, you know."

"No, trust me. It's not an actual D&D game. It's really fun. I think you'll like it. Plus, it will keep your mind off everything." She looked at me. "And that's what we want right now. We don't want you to have too much time to sit around moping and thinking about you know who."

"I guess, but I was thinking maybe we could watch a movie on Netflix. Or I know—the new season of *Love is Blind* is out."

"The last thing you need to watch is a reality TV show about dating."

"I've actually seen some of the season," Shantal said, "and the guys are total jerks. So perhaps it will make you feel better."

"Or worse." I made a face. "I don't want to deal with anymore jerks. I just want to meet some guy that makes me believe in true love and that there's going to be a happily ever after."

"Well, you've met Finn," Marcia said.

"Yeah, Finn's great."

"Why does it sound like you don't actually believe that?"

"No, I do. He's great and I'm happy for you, but how realistic is it going to be that I'm going to also meet a handsome billionaire that wants to whisk me away and marry me?"

"I know, right?" Lilian said, shaking her head. "Let's be real. We'd be lucky to meet guys that can pay their own rent."

"I know," I said with a laugh. "But I can't talk, because I can't even pay my own rent myself."

"Oh yeah," Marcia said. "By the way..."

"What?"

"Finn wants to know if you can start on Monday."

"Oh, the training position?"

"Yeah. Heads up, though. Gloria is the one that's going to be doing your documents."

"Oh no, not the Gloria that was the HR rep you dealt with."

"Yep. She's okay, but..."

"No, she's not." Shantal said. "I can't stand her."

"Me neither," Lilian said. "But I guess it's a rite of passage when you work there. You have to deal with Gloria."

"Oh, yay. Well, I don't have any other good offers right now, so I guess I'll take it. I mean I'd rather work for Finn than listen to guys jack off all day." I sighed. "Okay, shall we go sit at the dining room table and play this board game?"

"Yep," Lilian said. "And trust me, it's fun. If you're not enjoying it after twenty minutes, we'll watch TV or something."

"Okay, sounds like a plan."

"I'm kind of hungry," Marcia said. "Can we order pizza?"

"Ooh. Yeah, let's get Italian," Shantal said. "I really want spaghetti and meatballs."

"I can just make some spaghetti and meatballs," I said, shaking my head.

"No, you're not going to cook for us. We're playing a game, and you're getting over your disappointment," Marcia said. "I should've known that Brody was going to be an asshole. I feel so responsible for this bullshit. I'm sorry."

"Girl, it's not your fault."

"It is. If it weren't for me, you wouldn't have gone. And if it weren't for me dating Finn, then he wouldn't have brought Brody. Then he wouldn't have gotten your hopes up, and you wouldn't be sad."

"I'm not sad. I'm okay."

"Really?" She stared at the half-eaten box of chocolates that was on the table. "You're really not sad?"

"Just because I'm eating my weight in chocolates doesn't mean I'm really, really upset. If I had also eaten two gallons of ice cream, then maybe."

"So if he does call you, will you speak to him?" Lilian asked curiously.

"No, I'm done. I'm not playing these games with him. In the past, I've given guys plenty of chances, and there's not been one guy that's been worth it." I paused. "And after saying all that, if he calls again, maybe I will speak to him because I have a big heart and well, you know."

"Yeah, I feel you." Lilian sighed. "I just don't understand why guys play games. All he had to do was text you and let you know that he wasn't going to make it."

"Exactly. Just a little courtesy, a little respect. But no, he didn't respect me at all."

"I'm sorry," Shantal said. "I've dated baseball players before. Well, one baseball player in high school, who is now a drug addict, but long story short, he was the same way."

"What?" Lilian said. "You need to tell us that story."

"He played on the varsity baseball team. He was really, really cute. His name was Cameron. He kind of looked like... Oh my God, what's the actor's name?"

Lilian frowned. "Ryan Reynolds?"

"No, not Ryan Reynolds. Does Ryan Reynolds look like a baseball player to you?"

"I don't know." Lilian shook her head. "Bradley Cooper."

"No, not Bradley Cooper. This guy has dark hair."

"Henry Cavill?"

Shantal laughed. "I wish."

"Ben Affleck?"

"No, Ben Affleck's old."

"Well, you're not that young yourself."

"I'm not in my fifties."

"Neither is Ben Affleck," Lilian said. Marcia and I just looked at each other and smiled as the two babbled on about different actors.

"You sure you're okay?" Marcia said softly as we moved the board game to the table.

"Yeah. I'm a little upset and disappointed, and I guess I'm confused, but who understands men, right? Sometimes I really do feel like we're living on two different planets. And it sucks because I really thought that he and I were finally going to make some headway, you know? I thought that my friendship mattered to him, but obviously it doesn't. If it did, he would've showed up or he would've contacted me."

"I think he has a lot of growing up to do," Marcia said. "And while that's generally the case for all men, it doesn't seem like he's going to be maturing anytime soon. I think you're smart. Just ignore him if he messages you again. We'll find you a much better guy."

"Thanks, Marcia. You're great."

"No, girl. You're great. Now come on, let me beat you at this board game."

TWENTY-SIX

Brody

"It's four o'clock somewhere." I picked up my beer mug and chugged. "Somewhere over the rainbow." I held my hand up to the bartender, who was pouring vodka into a glass.

"It's actually ten o'clock." He shook his head. "You've been here all day."

"My money's good."

"Yeah, but is your liver?" He handed the vodka to the cute chick standing next to me. "Ten dollars, doll."

"I got it." I held my hand up and beamed at her. "Hi, I'm Brody."

"Hi, I'm Yoko." She smiled as she ignored my hand. "You didn't have to buy my drink."

"Anything for a pretty girl like you." I looked at her long black hair and nodded. "You got some long hair, girl."

"Secret is, I never cut it." She grinned and held up her glass. "Cheers."

"Cheers to you too." I sipped more of my beer and then hiccuped. "My girl... Oops, I mean my friend has black hair as well."

I could see the light going off in Yoko's eyes.

"Okay, that's nice."

"She might not even be my friend right now." I hiccuped again. "I stood her up for breakfast."

"That's not very nice."

"I'm not very nice." I slammed my mug down and started singing. "In Dublin's fair city..."

"Can you keep it down?" The bartender stopped in front of me again. "I think you've had enough. Maybe you should go home."

"Go home? I've got no home. Plus, Yoko and I—" I looked to the side, but my new friend was gone. "Well, I've got women to impress and balls to throw." I threw my head back and started laughing. "I wish I could throw my blue balls away as well. Fuck, I'm horny as hell."

"Dude, do you have someone I can call?" The bartender was frowning now. "You're not good for business."

"Well, you can't call my brother Michael because he's an asshole and won't answer. He should be taking care of his kids, but instead he's fucking his high school girlfriend, who I fucked when I was in college. He's a fucking tool. And you can't call my brother Patrick either."

The bartender pressed his lips together.

"You wanna know why you can't call him?"

He sighed. "Why?"

"Because he's fucking dead." I stared at him, waiting to see his reaction. My head was pounding, and I was exhausted. "He's fucking in the ground or heaven or wherever dead people fucking go."

I pointed at him. "What's your name?"

"Rio." He tapped his fingers against the bar, and I found the sound oddly comforting.

"Well, Rio, where is it that dead people go? Do they go to heaven? Hell? Rot in the ground? Fucking assholes. They think they can just leave us here."

"Mr. Wainwright." He leaned forward. "Please, can I call someone for you?"

"You can't call Susie. I bet she hates my fucking guts." I shook my head. "She didn't hate me when I was eating her out, though. The way she squirmed and squealed..." I laughed. "She loved it." My words hit me like a ton of bricks and I pressed my mouth shut. This was not the way a man spoke about a woman he cared about. I was far to immature to appreciate that Susie was a woman that deserved the best.

And then for a few seconds, sobering thoughts passed through me. Susie. I'd stood her up. No call. No text. No nothing. I grabbed my phone and powered it on. Dozens of texts and voicemails came through, and I saw that there were several from Susie. I was an asshole. It suddenly struck me that this was my defining moment. This was the moment I knew I had to grow up. I didn't want this life anymore. I didn't want strange women. Or seedy bars. Or nights that I couldn't remember. I wanted love. I wanted what Finn had. I wanted a warm smile on a cold day that reminded me that there was good in the world. I wanted Susie.

"I'm an asshole," I said loudly. "I'm a fucking asshole."

"Yes, you are. Now shut the fuck up," a young guy sitting behind me shouted. "What the hell, man?"

I handed my phone to Rio and placed my head on the countertop. It smelled of stale beer and nuts, and it was starting to make me feel nauseous. "Call Finn. He'll come and get me. Good ol' Finn."

"YOU LOOK LIKE SHIT." Finn sounded pissed as I opened my eyes. I sat up and realized I was on his couch.

"Shit. What time is it?" I rubbed my forehead. I had a splitting headache. "I need some aspirin and water. And food."

"What the hell is going on with you, man?" Finn sat on the couch next to me. "You were completely out of it when I got to the bar last night."

"Oh yeah, I was at the bar. What happened to Yoko?"

"Who?"

"The girl I was..." I started to grin but stopped when I saw the look on Finn's face. I didn't know why I was faking being Mr. big man on campus. "You're mad at me?"

"You stood Susie up. You didn't call her or text her. A bartender calls me in the middle of the night to tell me that NY's number one baseball player is in his bar, drunk off his ass, and that people are taking photos. I'm not only mad. I'm pissed as hell. What the hell is going on, Brody? And don't tell me nothing. I won't believe you."

"Since when do you want to have deep conversations?" I closed my eyes and sat back.

"I'm your best friend." He grabbed me by the shoulders. "What the hell is going on?"

I slowly opened my eyes and stared past his shoulders at the wall behind him. My vision blurred, and my head was pounding. I could feel myself getting emotional, and my eyes were starting to water. I jumped up quickly. Like hell I was going to cry in front of Finn.

"I know I fucked up. I know that I've been an immature bastard. I want Susie, Finn. I want her to know she's special to me and I just don't know what to do." I laid my cards on the table and waited for him to respond. There was a light in his eyes that I hadn't seen before and he suddenly smiled.

"I told you this day would come."

"What?"

"The day you'd fall hard." He grinned. "And yes, you have been a major fool and yes, you have some growing up to do, but you're on the right track."

"Do you think I have a chance?"

"I have no idea." He shook his head. "But let's brainstorm and come up with some ideas."

"Okay." I nodded. "In ten minutes? I think I need a shower first."

"Fine. Take one and then we talk." He jumped up as well. "Susie and Marcia are both worried about you and me as well."

"What did you tell them?"

"That you were sleeping off a hangover."

"She's going to hate me."

"I wouldn't be surprised if she did." He nodded.

"Can you call her? Ask her to come over?"

"Susie?" He raised an eyebrow. "Really?"

"If I'm going to talk, it's only going to be once, and I want her to be there."

"Fine." He sighed. "I'll ask her, but you know she might not come."

"I know, but it's worth a try." I sighed as I headed toward the bathroom. I turned on the water and made sure it was set to cold. I needed freezing water to wake me up and get me out of the trance I'd found myself in. I suddenly had a thought and opened the bathroom door and yelled,

"Can you also get as many papers as you can today? I want to see if I made the news."

"On it," Finn shouted back.

"Oh and I had an idea." I said as a thought hit me.

"What's the idea?"

"Do you think you can help me get a singing telegram?"

"A what?" Finn looked confused.

"Just Google it." I laughed. "I'll tell you more when I am out of the shower."

And with that, I closed the door and jumped under the gushing cold water. I stood there for five minutes, letting the water drench me. My stomach was twisted in knots. I knew the day of reckoning was finally here, and I had no idea how I was going to cope.

The doorbell rang as I was playing a game on my phone, and I felt too lazy to move.

"Can you get that, Marcia?"

"I'm in the bathroom, so no."

I huffed as I got off of the couch. I was not in the mood for anything today. I peeked through the hole, but it was blocked by something red. I let out a deep sigh and opened the door.

"Yes, can I help you?" There was a man standing there in a suit, holding a bunch of balloons and a box of chocolates."

"Are you, Susie?"

"Uh, yes. Why?"

The man handed me the balloons and chocolates and pulled out his phone. All of a sudden some classical music started playing and he gave me a quick bow. I gawked at him and watched as he straightened up and pulled a card out of his pocket.

"Sorry, I normally memorize these, but this was last minute and very long." He shrugged. "A one, a two, a one, two...Susie Benedict, I am a fool. I stood you up and it wasn't cool. I've made so many mistakes, I think it's only fair, that you ignore me; even though I have good hair. I think you're beautiful, I love your smile. The sun rises and shines, but it's not brighter than the look in your eyes. I know I'm an idiot, I know I'm immature, but I'm begging for you to give me just one more, one more chance to show you, I can be a better man. Just one more chance to show you, that I can change. I have things I want to tell you. Try to explain why. Please do me the honor of coming to my side. I'm not a writer as good as you, but this is from my heart and all I could do." The man took a deep breath and bowed again.

"This is a singing telegram from Brody Wainwright." He smiled at me and I just stared at him with wide eyes and twitching lips.

"What in the world?" I wasn't sure what else to say.

"I'm guessing Mr. Brody is a guy that messed up huh?" The man in the suit shrugged. "Maybe hear what he has to say? If he's still a douche, just leave?"

"True." I smiled. "It doesn't hurt to listen."

"It truly doesn't. You have a nice day, Susie." He bowed again and then he was gone. I closed the door behind me and stared at the ten balloons in my hand and the box of Godiva chocolate. It obviously wasn't enough to make me forgive Brody, but it was a start. I opened the box of chocolates and popped one in my mouth. Brody Wainwright was a complex man, but I was starting to think that maybe he was a lot deeper than he'd ever let on.

"I REALLY DON'T KNOW if I should be going, but I guess I want some answers," I said to Marcia as we made our way up to Finn's apartment. This was going to be the first time I'd actually gone to his apartment, and I was excited to see it, though I was more confused as to why Brody had summoned me there.

"I know. You really don't have to go," Marcia said, squeezing my hand. "I told Finn that Brody's expecting a lot, and he doesn't deserve it. He's done nothing for you to forgive him."

"I know, but if I don't go and listen, then I'll always wonder what happened, you know? And I don't just want to hear it from Finn. I'd kind of like to hear it from Brody's own mouth."

"I know," she said. "I'd be the same way. It's just that he sucks. Finn had to go pick him up from a bar. He was drunk off his rocker, barely conscious. The bartender said he'd been there all day."

"All day?" I stared at her in surprise. "So instead of coming to take me to breakfast, he went to the bar?"

"I guess so. He's some sort of lush or something. I told Finn that perhaps he should be going to AA."

"Is he an alcoholic?"

"I don't know. I know him as much as you do. In fact, I know him less than you do. But something just doesn't seem right."

"I know, but hopefully it'll make sense when he tells us."

"Yeah, I guess." She shrugged. "I mean, honestly, it just sounds like he's still living that young man lifestyle; both mentally and physically. Maybe he thinks he's a P I M P pimp."

"What?"

"Hey, those aren't my words. Those are the words in the rap songs."

"Which rap song are you talking about?"

"You know what I mean."

"I guess," I said. "But let's give him a chance, yeah?"

"Why and how are you so understanding? You have the patience of a saint."

"Not really. I kind of want to slap him and scream at him, but I'll do that after he tells us what's up."

"Good idea." We finally made it outside Finn's door, and she knocked.

"Oh, I thought he gave you a key?"

"He did." She grinned. "But I don't want to seem too familiar."

"Doesn't he want you to move in? How is you opening the door with the key that he gave you too familiar?"

"Yeah, he loves me. And yeah, he wants to be with me, but I'm worried that if I start showing I'm too eager, he's going to get cold feet."

"No, he's not."

"Trust me. Every guy gets cold feet. They love the chase, and once they've got you, well... You've got to always keep things new and different."

"What do you mean?"

"You've got to keep them on their toes," she said. "Play a little hard to get sometimes."

"Marcia, you do not play hard to get with Finn whatsoever."

"Okay, okay. So I haven't actually started following through on those rules yet."

"Hey," Finn said as he opened the door. He leaned down and gave Marcia a kiss on the lips. "Why didn't you use your key?"

"I didn't want to walk in, just in case you or Brody were naked."

"Um, why would we be walking around naked?" he said, staring at her.

"I don't know," she said. "Maybe it's a guy thing."

"No, it's not. Come in. Hey, Susie," he said, looking at me. "Thanks for coming. I know you probably didn't want to, but I think it will mean a lot to Brody."

"Yeah. I mean, honestly, I just came because I want to know why he stood me up, you know?"

"Yeah, I know," he said. "And hopefully he has a good answer for that."

"Oh, you don't know why?"

"No. I asked him what his explanation was, and he said he didn't want to say anything until you were here because he only wanted to tell the story once."

"That's so he doesn't forget his lies," Marcia said.

"I don't think so," Finn said seriously. "I think whatever he has to tell us, it's important." He sighed. "So try not to be too hard on him, okay? At least, not until after he's spoken."

"Yeah, sure." I looked around the apartment. "What a stunning view. Oh my gosh," I said as I hurried over to the window. "Is that the Chrysler Building? And that's Central Park? Wow. This is absolutely amazing. You're so lucky, Marcia."

"It's okay." She grinned. "I actually kind of want him to move."

"What, why?"

"You know," she said. "History."

"What?"

"She doesn't like the fact that I've had other women here," he said, rolling his eyes. "But none of them were special. None of them..."

"It doesn't matter if they were special or not. I don't like thinking that the bed I'm sharing with you is a bed you've shared with other women."

"I can just change the bed."

"Yeah, but I don't want to think about you with other women at all."

"Fine, Marcia. We can look for another place." And then we heard someone clearing their throat. I looked up and it was Brody. He looked like shit. Handsome still, of course, but like shit. His eyes were red, and his face was pale. He was wearing a pair of gray sweatpants and a white T-shirt, and he was staring directly at me.

"Hey, Susie," he said, his voice gruff and soft, and he walked toward me. I didn't smile, and I didn't even respond. "I'm really sorry about yesterday. I should have texted or called."

"Yeah, you should have. I texted you and I called you, and you didn't even bother responding."

"I turned my phone off."

"Before or after I texted or called?" He took a deep breath and sighed. I watched as he ran his hands through his hair and counted to three. I wondered what that was about.

"I got you some roses, you know."

"Oh, where are they?" I looked around the apartment.

"I left them on a park bench." He sighed. "So I guess that doesn't really count, huh?"

"Nope."

"I got you three different colors. I think yellow and purple and pink, or maybe red. I can't remember."

"Okay?"

"They all symbolize different things, you know?"

"Yep, I've heard that."

"One was for friendship, and one was for passion, and—"

"Brody," Finn interrupted him. "I'm not trying to be a dick here, but I don't think Susie cares about the roses you got for her and don't actually have."

"I know. I just wanted you to know," he said, staring at me.

"Yeah. I didn't come here for small talk. Finn said that whatever you had to say, you wanted to say in front of me as well. So I figured I'd come, because I don't want to be eighty years old wondering, 'Oh, whatever happened with that one dude, Brody Wainwright? Why didn't he show up that day?'"

"You think you'll be thinking about me when you're eighty years old?" His lips twitched and he smiled.

"No," I said, glaring at him.

"Okay. I guess I deserve that. Shall we have a seat?"

"Yeah."

"I made some coffee." Finn looked around the room. "Anyone else want some?"

"I would love some," Brody answered.

"Me too," I said.

"Okay. Marcia, help me?"

"You got it."

They headed toward what I assumed was the kitchen, and I went to the living room couch and sat down. Brody sat down next to me and grabbed my hands. I pulled them away quickly.

"Please don't."

"You're pissed off at me, huh?"

"Yeah, you think?" I said, glaring at him. "You made a breakfast date with me, you didn't show up, and you didn't even call to cancel or text me? I was worried sick about you, and I was upset. I didn't know what happened. And you know what, Brody? Like, this is all just a lot. You were an asshole when we went camping. You were an asshole on the phone. I was finally going to give you a chance, and then you were a fucking asshole again. Like, what do you want from me? I'm done giving you chances."

"I'm sorry."

"You know what? Sorry doesn't cut it. Sorry doesn't make me feel better. Sorry doesn't give me back the hours I spent wasted, worrying, calling freaking hospitals and police stations."

"You called hospitals?" There was a light in his eyes.

"Yeah. Like I said, I was worried."

"I didn't mean to make you worry."

"You didn't care."

"I did. I... I was selfish, and I was only thinking about myself." He sat back. "I know there's nothing I can say or do to make up for everything, but I do owe you an explanation, and I hope once you hear my explanation, you can find it in your heart to forgive me and..." He shrugged. "I don't know."

"Yeah, well, we'll see." I looked up as Finn and Marcia walked back into the room with cups of coffee. I smiled when I saw that Marcia also had a plate with croissants on it. "Thanks, girl."

"You're welcome." She placed them down on the coffee table and then sat on the other side of the room in a small leather chair. Finn went and stood by the window and sipped on his coffee.

"Okay, whenever you're ready, Brody." Finn prodded.

Brody stood up and started pacing the floor in the living room. "Before I say anything else, I contacted my agent. There's a publisher who wants me to write a book." He stared at me. "And they are looking for other authors as well, debut authors. I told him I knew someone...who was talented...who deserved a chance. He would love to meet up with you next week, if you're free."

"You didn't have to do that." I was shocked at what he'd done and didn't even know if I could or should accept.

"I would do anything to make your dreams come true." He said softly and there was a fire in his eyes as he gazed at me. "I know I haven't done much to show you that I can be a good guy, but...I want to." He sighed. "But I guess you need to understand some things first." He choked up slightly.

"I'm listening." I could feel my resolve weakening as I realized just how emotional this was for him. I had a feeling he'd never been in such a vulnerable position before in his life.

"This is kind of hard for me to talk about," he said, "and honestly, I never thought that I would, but I owe all of you an explanation." He looked at Finn.

"You're my best friend, and you've always been by my side. You've always had my back, and I owe you the truth." He turned to Marcia. "You're Finn's girl. I've disrespected you, and I've disrespected your best friend. And for that, I apologize."

And then he looked at me. I could feel my heart racing as I saw the sincerity in his eyes. He headed toward me, then crouched down on the ground in front of me and grabbed my hand. This time, I didn't pull away.

"And you, Susie. I don't know what to say actually. You've touched a part of me I didn't know existed. You've given me something I never thought I would feel again."

He stopped then and took a deep breath. "I'm starting to feel overwhelmed. This isn't usually how I operate." He jumped back up. "So, I guess I'll start at the beginning.

Maybe if you have questions, guys, you'll save them till the end?"

"Okay," I said and nodded. Finn and Marcia nodded as well.

"So I grew up in Pennsylvania, and my grandparents lived in Kentucky. I had an older brother, Michael, and a younger brother, Patrick, and we were all pretty close. Though, Michael and Patrick were best friends. They could have been clones."

He shook his head. "They were into exactly the same things—playing football, baseball, soccer, basketball. They used to like to go foraging and shooting. Wherever Michael was, Patrick was as well. Michael was a football player, but Patrick... He was a baseball player. He had a real gift. Everyone talked about it. Everyone knew it. We all expected him to go pro when he was older. He was fearless. He was the baby of the family, yet he could do anything he wanted. And he and Michael lived life that way."

"You weren't the star baseball player?" Marcia said, and then she pressed her hand against her mouth. "Sorry, I forgot we're not meant to speak."

"No, it's okay. And no, I hated sports when I was young. I couldn't throw a ball to save my life. I couldn't even hit a ball. I hated football and I hated basketball. I was always with my books. My grams, you see, she'd wanted a granddaughter. And I guess she'd wanted someone to knit and crochet and share a love of reading with.

"Well, I wasn't into crocheting or knitting or anything like that, but I love to read. And so, she'd share her favorite books with me, and I'd spend my days reading and doing little science projects. I had a book of bird and butterfly classifications, and I'd walk around the farm and name every insect and every bird that I'd see, then I'd write it down in a little black journal."

He laughed. "Ironic, huh? My first black journal wasn't for girls' names or women that I wanted to be with or had been with. It was on insects I found on my grandparents' farm. Of course, my brothers teased me for it. I was the nerd of the family. And of course, when I was in school, I was teased because I wasn't a *real* Wainwright. How could I be a Wainwright if I wasn't into sports? Michael had paved the way for all of us, being the genius that he was. He was the sports star, and then came me. But it didn't matter so much because there was Patrick. Patrick was great and everyone talked about him. And I didn't mind, not really. Until one day, when there was this girl."

"There's always a girl," Finn said, shaking his head. Brody nodded and then looked at me.

"Yep. There's always a girl that changes everything. I liked her, you know? I wanted to ask her out. I thought I had a shot. But she laughed and her friends laughed, and pretty much everyone in school laughed about the fact that I could possibly think a geek like me would get to date a popular, beautiful girl like her. And then I got angry, because I was a Wainwright. I was the same as Michael and Patrick. Everyone said it. We all looked the same, and we came from the same DNA, yet they were popular and I was no one. We went to my grandparents' farm, and I was seething and ignoring them. And they wanted to go chop firewood or something."

"Oh?" I said softly as he stopped. He looked off into the distance, and it was as if he was back in that moment. I watched a gamut of emotions cross his face, and he shook his head as if to clear his thoughts.

"I had this idea that we could pretend to be Tarzan. I

don't know why. Maybe I wanted to prove to them that I was a man as well, that I could do manly things and didn't just have to have a book in my hands. I don't know. But I remember Patrick... He took the axe and..." He paused, his voice cracking.

"Are you okay, Brody?" Marcia said softly. I looked over at her, surprised. I could see sadness and worry in her face, and I realized she was just as touched as I was by his story.

Finn walked over to Brody and put his arm around his shoulder. "Dude, if it's too much, you don't have to continue."

"No, I want to," he said, and then he came and sat by me. "I never thought I'd tell this story to anyone. But since meeting you... Well, anyway. We went out into the forest, and we were swinging on vines. Don't ask what vines. I can't even remember now. I think it was branches that were hanging. But in my eyes, they were vines. I was a teenage boy, you know?"

"Yeah," I said, "I get it. The imagination is a wonderful place."

"And then there was this tree." He chewed on his lower lip. "And we decided to have a competition. We decided to see who could climb the highest. And of course, I wanted to prove myself, and so I climbed and climbed and climbed so high. Michael stopped. He wouldn't admit it, but he was kind of scared of heights, so he gave up first. But Patrick... Oh, Patrick was fearless, and he climbed that tree with me. He wasn't going to let me beat him. We got up high, and he was doing great. He was going to beat me. But I..."

His voice choked. "I decided to go out on a limb that I shouldn't have, and then it started to break, and Patrick, well, even though he was the youngest, he was the super-hero of the family. He said, 'Grab my hand.' And I said, 'I can't, it's too far.' And I should have taught him to stop. I should have..."

I could see tears welling in his eyes, and he started sobbing. "He fell. He fell. It must have been twenty feet, thirty feet... I don't even know how high. All I can remember is Michael's scream. I don't even know how I did it, but I got off that limb and I clambered down. It must have been the adrenaline or the shock. I don't know what. And I just remember seeing his face—innocent, young—and his limbs all twisted, and he wasn't breathing. And his head was cracked, and it was bleeding, and he wasn't breathing. I tried to drop to my knees and give him mouth to mouth, but it didn't matter. And Michael just stood there and... It was horrible. He was dead. The doctors say probably on impact."

He looked at me then. "And I carry it. I carry it to this day. I killed my brother."

"You didn't kill him. Oh my gosh, Brody, you can't carry that with you. You didn't..."

"I did. If it wasn't for me having to prove myself, for me feeling like a loser..." He jumped up. "So I finished out high school, and of course my parents hated me and Michael hated me, and some words were said."

"What words were said?" I asked him. I jumped up and walked over to him and grabbed his hands. I pulled him to me. "Look at me, Brody. What words were said?"

I knew it would probably hurt him to tell me, but if they were negative, he needed someone to counteract them. He needed someone to tell him that those words weren't true.

"My parents said that it should have been me, and Michael agreed."

"Oh, my word. No, Brody. How could they say that? That's horrible. It's..."

"They regretted it. I mean, I never spoke to them really after that. When your parents tell you that they wish you would've died... It was in grief, of course, but I never forgave myself. And so when I started college, I remember walking around, looking at the different clubs, and the baseball team had tryouts. Walk-ons. I'd never heard of such a thing. I went, and that's where I met Finn on the first day."

"But you were amazing, dude." Finn looked at him. "You seemed like you'd been playing baseball your entire life."

Brody shrugged. "Funny, isn't it?"

"I don't know what to say."

He took a deep breath. "These demons have been in me for a long time. And this guilt and pain... it's been the driving force behind my life. I figured if Patrick couldn't be the star baseball player, then I would be. If Patrick couldn't get all the women, then I would get all the women. I'd do it all for him. I'd make him happy. But it hasn't made me happy, and I try to shut it all out. I don't like to think about it because it just hurts me so badly. And every time I think about him, every time I see his face, then I don't see the fun, happy guy that I spent so many years with. I see my dead brother lying on the ground. I see the life gone out of him all because of me, and I hear my older brother's screams, and I just want to go back to that day. I just want to change what happened."

He was shouting now. "I don't know what I could have done differently. I don't know..." I grabbed him then and pulled him toward me, and he started sobbing. I felt my shoulder getting wet as he cried, and I rubbed his back. Marcia jumped up and walked over to us and rubbed his back as well.

Finn stood to the side of us, looking sad. "I'm sorry, Brody. I had no idea."

"I know." He lifted his head and smiled at me and then took a step back. "All these years, I've been carrying this. I know it's not healthy, and I know the lifestyle I've been living isn't good, and I guess it's all come to a head. I guess just too many things in the past couple of weeks have brought it to my mind, and yesterday..." He stared at me. "Yesterday, I bought you some roses, and I was so happy to go to breakfast with you because I wanted to tell you how much I liked you, and I wanted to tell you that our time camping had been the best time of my life.

"But then these two boys ran up to me, and they wanted my autograph. And at first it was cool, but their names were Michael and Patrick, like my brothers. As I stared at the young boys' faces—as I stared at Patrick's face—I remembered my younger brother and how innocent he had been as well. It all came crashing down, and I knew I didn't deserve to find happiness. I didn't deserve to be with a woman like you, because Patrick, he would never get to be with someone that he's falling in love with." He paused. "Fuck it. I didn't mean to say that."

"You didn't mean to say it because it's not true?"

"No, I didn't mean to say it, because I don't deserve you, Susie."

"But is it true? Are you falling in love with me?"

"From the first time I saw your beautiful smile, and then when you told me that I was an asshole and a jerk, and then the way you kissed me... I knew. I'd never felt something like that before. I'd never met a woman that delighted me, that made me laugh, that made me angry, that made me talk so much. I'm not a talker, and here I am."

He shook his head. "But I don't deserve you, Susie, and

you don't deserve to be with someone like me, who has so many demons. I was drunk all day yesterday. I went from the park to the bar, and I must have drunk fifteen beers and had shots.

"I'm fucked up. To the world, I'm Brody Wainwright, pitcher for the New York Yankees. Handsome, rich, with women falling out of his pockets. To the world, I have everything, and yet I have nothing. I'm cold inside. I feel dead inside. Don't you understand? And then I met you, and I started to feel again. I started to want to be more than the guy that just made jokes to save face. That just made jokes to stop anyone from getting too close. You got close, Susie. You got close, and I couldn't take it, and I'm sorry. And I just want you to understand how much you mean to me. I want you to understand that you are the most special, most beautiful woman I've ever met, and you deserve the world."

"Maybe you are the world to me, Brody." I took a step forward and squeezed his hand. "Maybe I'm kind of falling for you as well."

"But," he said, "you—"

"I think I get to make up my mind on if I deserve you or not." I smiled and wiped the tears away from his face and gave him a quick kiss on the lips. "You don't have to carry this guilt, Brody. You were young and it wasn't your fault. It's not your fault your brother fell. It's not your fault your brother passed. I know you don't feel that way, and I know you will always regret what happened, but you have to figure out a way to work through this, and I can be there with you. I can be there for you if you want me to," I said softly. "I'm sorry that you've been triggered all these times, but there are ways to deal with that. I promise."

"Would you really be willing to give me a chance?" His eyes lit up as he stared at me. "I have a lot of growing to do and I have to figure out...well, you know, learn to deal with my guilt, but having you by my side...it would mean the world to me."

"I'm here for you, Brody." I stared at him for a few seconds. "I can't believe I'm able to forgive everything so quickly, but sometimes..."

"When you know you know." He kissed me softly on the lips. "I don't deserve you, Susie, but I'm willing to spend the rest of my life showing you how hard I will work to deserve your heart. I want to make you the happiest woman on earth because you've already made me the happiest man and you've shown me that I don't have to hide my feelings or pretend to be someone I'm not just to stop the hurt."

"We will always be triggered or hurt by people or events." I said softly. "But it's how we deal with those inter-actions that determines our fate. We are the only ones we have to worry about. Protect your heart; but be open to all the love that is out there. Be open to my love."

"I've been waiting my entire life for a love like yours Susie. I just never knew it.'

TWENTY-EIGHT

BRODY

"Susie, you don't know what you're saying. You..."

"I do know what I'm saying." She nodded and gave me the sweetest smile I'd ever seen in my life. "This is not your fault, Brody. I promise you, it wasn't your fault."

"You don't understand. If I wasn't trying to prove myself. If I..." I could hear my voice cracking as my heart broke. I couldn't believe that I'd gone back to that day. I hated thinking about it. I hated thinking about that moment, being high up in that tree and watching him fall as if in slow motion. Seeing his face so young, so innocent, and how the blood seeped into the ground.

"Brody." Susie squeezed my hand. "Stop thinking about it."

My eyes flickered to hers in surprise. "How did you know?"

"I can tell. It's healthy for you to talk about it. It's healthy for you to process everything, but you can't internalize it, okay? You have to talk it through and understand that you were a young boy too. And you couldn't have known."

"If I hadn't gone onto that limb, if I'd just been safer, if he hadn't reached his hand to help me..." I shook my head. "I just replay all these ifs. If I'd done this, if I hadn't done that, if he..."

I looked up at the ceiling. "And I miss him, you know? I miss him. Sometimes I wake up in the middle of the night, and I think to myself, 'Oh, I've got to tell Patrick about this baseball story,' and then it hits me all over again that I can't tell him."

"You can, you know," Susie said.

"What do you mean?"

"I believe that our loved ones are out there looking over us, and I believe that you can still talk to them. And if you listen closely, they'll answer."

"Really? Well, I've been talking to him for a long time, and he hasn't answered anything."

"That's not true," Finn said, shaking his head. "You're a baseball star now, right? You don't think some of your brother's in you?"

"True," I said, nodding. "It's weird because I was always shit at sports when I was young. That's why I never really got into it, and because I was so much more interested in science. And, well, when I stepped onto that field in college, it was like I was possessed almost. I mean, I don't think I was. Please God, I hope I wasn't." I chuckled, and Susie smiled. "But sometimes I do think he's with me."

I sighed. "I guess it's not only his death I feel bad about, I feel like I ruined my family as well. My parents? Well, they never got over it. And my older brother is an issue all by himself."

"You can't take that on," Susie said. "You can only worry about yourself and take care of your own wellbeing. And you're a good guy, Brody, or I wouldn't be here."

"You're just saying that," I said, shaking my head. "You think I'm a jerk. You can admit it. You've already told me you wouldn't be with me if I was the last man on earth."

"Well, no. I said I wouldn't sleep with you if you were the last man on earth." Her eyes twinkled. "And, you know, perhaps that's not quite true."

"Oh, really?"

"Really, Brody. That's what's going to get you smiling?" she said with a giggle.

"No, but I think we've had enough serious talk for the morning. I wanted to explain everything because I thought it was important. And I hope you understand that I'm being sincere to all of you."

"I think you are sincere. Man, I wish I would've known. You're my brother, dude. And I'll do anything for you. I'll always be here for you. You know that, right?"

"I know. That's why I told the bartender to call you last night." I looked at Susie and saw the apprehension in her face. "I didn't do anything at the bar. Just drank. Didn't hook up. Didn't make out. Didn't get any numbers. Didn't even ask for any numbers."

"I didn't ask."

"I know you didn't, but I just wanted you to know. And same in LA. I didn't do anything."

"Okay," she said.

"And what about you?"

"What do you mean what about me?"

"I mean, I don't care, obviously. Well, that's not true. I do care. But I'm not going to be pissed, because I don't have the right to be. But I'd like to know. Did you kiss anyone this weekend?"

"You mean when I went clubbing?"

"Yeah, or any other time."

"I've kissed men before in my life."

"Yeah, I know that. I'm not an idiot." Though a part of me wished I was the only one she'd ever kissed, I knew that was absolutely ridiculous. "So you want to grab something to eat? I owe you a breakfast."

"You do owe me a breakfast." She looked over at Finn and Marcia. "What are you guys up to?"

"You should go ahead," Marcia said, walking over to Finn and grabbing his arm. "We'll stay here."

"You sure?" Susie said.

"Yeah. I think you guys deserve some time alone." Marcia walked over to me and gave me a hug. "Thanks for telling us about your story, Brody. I know that must've taken a lot. And I agree with Susie. It's not your fault. And I also agree you're a good guy. We're here to listen, and we're here to help. Don't keep it in, okay?"

"Thanks," I said. "You're cool. I get why Finn loves you."

"Okay, boy," Finn said. "Stop trying to flatter my girl."

"Trust me, I'm just saying the truth. So breakfast?"

"Let's do it," Susie said, and we headed toward the door. "Bye, guys. I'll see you later."

"See you."

Susie and I walked out the front door and toward the elevator. I grabbed her hand and stared at her for a few seconds.

"I know this doesn't change anything, but..."

"Just kiss me, Brody," she said, bringing her face closer to mine. "Just shut up and kiss me." I grinned at her as I pressed her into the wall and placed my lips against hers. Her hands moved to my hair, and my hands wrapped around her waist as I devoured her, loving the feel of her, loving the taste of her, loving the touch of her. I wanted to consume her. I couldn't get enough of her.

And then I pulled away because I knew I was close to taking her right there, right in the corridor. And I knew that she wouldn't want that, especially not for our first time.

"Want to go get a hotel room?" I said, smiling at her. "I don't have my own place yet, and I figure we could order in breakfast?" I asked her hopefully.

"You want to order in breakfast? I thought we were going to go out for breakfast," she said playfully.

"We can go for breakfast, of course. I mean, I don't want to..."

"Let's go get a hotel room, Brody." She chewed on her lower lip. "Let's go now before I change my mind."

"Are you saying what I think you're saying?" I looked at her hopefully, and she nodded.

The elevator beeped, and then we walked inside. I pressed her against the back wall and started kissing her again. She murmured against my lips that I hadn't pressed the button to go down yet, and I laughed as I pulled away from her.

"Sorry, I just can't get enough of you right now."

"I can't get enough of you either, but we don't want to just stay in the elevator all day, do we?"

"I don't know." I shrugged. "I've never done it in an elevator before."

"You haven't?" she said, her eyes twinkling. "Why, I can't believe I've done something you haven't."

"Shut up." I stared at her. "You've had sex in an elevator?"

"No, but it was cool making you think I did."

"Oh my gosh, Susie Benedict." I shook my head. "I'm

going to take you right here, right now if you continue to tease me."

"Oh yeah?" She grinned at me and reached her hand to my crotch and squeezed. My cock responded, and she giggled delightfully.

"You can see I'm hard and ready. So if you're willing..."

She shook her head quickly. "We can't have sex in the elevator."

"But me thinks you're curious about it," I said, whispering in her ear.

She pulled away from me quickly as the elevated doors opened and two men walked in. They glanced at us for a couple of seconds and then pressed some buttons. She looked at me guiltily, and I just grinned at her.

I couldn't believe I was so lucky as to get a second, nay, third chance with Susie. And I also couldn't believe how freeing it felt to have told her and Finn and Marcia about that day with Patrick. And even though I wasn't fully healed, and even though the guilt still sat upon my heart, I started to believe what she said.

It wasn't my fault that he was dead. Yes, there were things I could've done differently that day. There were things I wish I could change. But it wasn't like I'd pushed him. It was wasn't like I'd killed him myself. He'd slipped and fallen, and fate had done its will.

I stared at her for a few seconds as we waited in the elevator, and I realized that there had been one thing I'd said that wasn't quite true. I told her that I was falling in love with her, but I knew as I stood there and stared at the way her lips curled up, and the way she played with her curly, dark hair, and the way that she kept giving me side glances, that I wasn't just falling in love with her. I was in love with her.

I was one hundred percent irrevocably in love with Susie Benedict, and I knew that I would do whatever it took to win her heart. I would do whatever it took to be the sort of man that she deserved to be with. As the men exited the elevator, I stepped toward her again and grabbed her hand.

"You're so beautiful."

"Where did that come from?" Her eyes narrowed. "I already told you I'd go to the hotel room with you."

"I know, but I just wanted to let you know. You are the most beautiful woman in the world, and I need to buy you some more roses."

"You don't have to buy me anymore roses. That's okay."

"I don't have to, but I want to. Or maybe I'll buy you your favorite flower. What's your favorite flower? Man, I don't even know your favorite flower."

"Well, there are many things you don't know about me, Brody, and there are many things I don't know about you. But that's what makes this all so exciting. We'll get to know everything."

"One thing I do know, Susie."

"What's that?"

"I know that I'm in love with you."

She gasped as she stared at me. "What did you just say?"

"I said I know I'm in love with you, and I know this will be the first time I've ever made love." I shook my head. "I can't believe it. I sound so corny. I sound like a douchebag, but it's true. I've never made love before and well..." I kissed the side of her face and whispered in her ear. "I can't wait to make love to you."

"I can't wait to make love to you as well," she whispered back. And then I pressed my lips against hers. I groaned as she once again squeezed my cock. And before I knew what was happening, I was hitting the emergency button and stopping the elevator. She glanced at me in surprise, and her twinkling eyes told me that she was down.

My hands ran up her shirt and cupped her breasts, and she moaned as I quickly pushed up her skirt and grabbed her and pressed her against the wall. She wrapped her legs around my waist, and I groaned in desire. My fingers moved to the inside of her thigh and slid her panties to the side before playing with her. She was wet and moaned as I touched her lightly and then more forcefully.

I slipped a finger inside of her and she gasped. I kissed her hard, and she kissed me back, her fingers digging into my scalp, pulling my hair. I loved the way she was so aggressive and so soft at the same time.

I reached down and unzipped my pants, and my cock sprang free. I pressed the head between her legs and thrust into her before she could even think. Her eyes blew open, and she gasped as I pummeled her.

"Oh fuck," she said, holding me close and kissing me again passionately. I thrust in and out of her, feeling like I was some sort of machine. My hands gripped her waist and hoisted her up higher. I pulled up her top and moved her bra down slightly so that I could suck on her nipples.

As I thrust into her, she cried out, "Oh, fuck. Brody, Brody. Oh my gosh." The sound of her voice saying my name took me over the top; I was about to come. I pumped into her a couple more times.

"Come for me, Susie. Come for me." And then she screamed, and I could feel a gush of wetness over my cock. And I thrust into her even faster and harder until I felt myself coming deep inside her.

I kissed her passionately as I pulled out and quickly zipped myself up. I put her panties back into place and slid her down so that she was standing on her own two feet. I quickly turned off the emergency button and pressed the lower level again and stared at her. She looked flushed and fucked and totally out of it.

"That was the fucking hottest thing I've ever done in my life," she said with a grin. And I knew then that I loved her even more than I thought possible.

"You're fucking sexy as hell. You know that, Susie?"

"Well, I should be. That was the fuck of my life." She laughed, and in that moment, I knew everything was going to work out perfectly.

She was literally the woman of my dreams.

"WHERE ARE WE GOING?" Susie questioned me as we headed towards Bleecker Street.

"It's a surprise."

"But I thought we were going to your hotel room."

"We will, but I promised you breakfast plus there was something else I wanted to give you."

"Not more balloons?" She giggled. "My apartment is filled with balloons right now."

"No, not more balloons." I squeezed her fingers. "Did I overdo it?"

"A little," She reached up and stopped me. She touched the side of my face and smiled. "The song was fun though. I can't believe you wrote that for me."

"Was that what convinced you to come and hear me out."

"Yes." She nodded. "I told myself I was going to make you sweat it out, but when I heard that song, well, I knew I had to come to hear you out. Even if I ended up leaving even more pissed off."

"I was a real jerk, huh?"

"I think you know the answer to that." She nodded. "Thankfully, our time in Yosemite showed me that underneath it all, there was a sweet, genuine man that was waiting to break out."

"So maybe you're a nature lover, after all."

"Maybe." She wrinkled her nose. "Please don't go booking any camping trips for us, though."

"I won't." I laughed. "At least not in the next 6 months or so."

"So where are we going?" She asked me after I gave her a quick kiss and started walking again.

"You'll see in a few minutes. Don't you like surprises?"

"I love them, actually." She admitted. "Especially surprise gifts."

"I'll remember that." Mentally I was already thinking about a bracelet I wanted to buy for her. It was a sterling silver charm bracelet and I wanted to add charms to celebrate each milestone of our relationship. I chuckled to myself as I realized that I'd never once in my life before thought about buying a woman a present. I suppose that was a sign of how much I loved her. "Okay, we're here."

"Magnolia Bakery?" She looked at me in surprise. "Why are we here?"

"Because I once read that taking a woman to Magnolia Bakery was one of the very first things you should do to show a woman you love her."

"Really?" Her eyes lit up as she gazed at me. "And you wanted to come now?"

"No time like the present, Susie." I pressed my lips against her forehead. "I want to spend every day of my life being a better man and showing you just how much you mean to me. I love you more than a fat kid loves cake." I started laughing. "Get it?"

"You're a goof, Brody, but I wouldn't have you any other way."

TWENTY-NINE
SUSIE

I lay on the luxurious linen sheet and looked up at Brody, who was grinning down at me. I was completely naked and so was he, and I giggled as he poured champagne on my body.

"You really shouldn't be wasting it, Brody. I would like to drink some."

"Well, how's about I lick it up, and you sip it from my mouth?"

"That doesn't sound quite as romantic or as sexy as you think it sounds. You know that, right?"

"It might not sound sexy, but it sure will be sexy," he said, winking as he fell onto the bed next to me. He leaned down and licked off the champagne he'd just poured onto my stomach , and my back arched as my entire body grew to life.

"You are really bad, Brody."

"I know," he said. "You know what I want to do tomorrow?"

"No. What do you want to do tomorrow?"

"I want to look for a house."

"You're going to look for a house? What?"

"I don't have anywhere to stay yet. And as I'm sure you know, I was kind of staying at Finn's and hotels. I'm ready to find a place, and I want you to help me. I want you to give me your womanly advice."

"Really? You trust me enough to let me help you choose a place?"

"Yeah. I want it to be someplace where you feel comfortable."

"Where I feel comfortable?" I blinked.

"I'm not asking you to move in with me right away, because that would be absolutely crazy." He paused. "Unless, of course, you want to move in with me."

"No, Brody. I can't move in with you. We don't really know each other that well."

"Yeah, but there's nothing like getting to know each other."

"Not while living with each other." I shook my head. "Plus, I want you to chase me. Just because I'm here with you right now, and I like you, and I'm in love with you, doesn't mean you still don't have to woo me."

"Oh, so you want to be wooed, do you?" He grinned at me, and I felt his hands playing with my hair.

"Yeah, I want to be wooed. I want to be treated like a princess."

"Don't worry, my dear. I will definitely treat you like a princess." He pressed his lips against mine, and his hands slid down my stomach between my legs. He started rubbing me fervently, and I moaned against his lips.

"And I don't just mean when it comes to the bedroom," I said, "even though that was pretty hot as well."

"What was pretty hot? Me doing you in the elevator or me doing you in the bed?"

"Both were pretty hot. Though I have to admit, I didn't think my first time making love with you was going to be in an elevator." I laughed. "But our relationship is anything but conventional."

"You're not mad at me, are you? I just couldn't resist. And I was so hot for you."

"No, it was perfect. It symbolizes what we have."

"And what's that?" he said.

"It's pure. It's raw. It's honest. It's dirty. It's impulsive. And it just doesn't make sense." I laughed. "But it works."

"It definitely works for me. How did I get so lucky to meet someone like you?"

"I don't know. Maybe you prayed to God for me?"

"Maybe," he said. He slipped a finger inside me, and I closed my eyes. "I just know that I never want to forget this feeling."

"What feeling is that?" I said, mumbling, barely coherent.

"This feeling of loving the person that I'm with. This feeling of contentment. This feeling of overwhelming happiness."

He slipped his finger out, and my eyes flew open. I pouted up at him. "Don't stop."

"Oh my darling, Susie. I'm going to give you something so much better than my finger," he said as he positioned himself between my legs.

His cock rubbed my clit, and I groaned. "Oh fuck," I said.

"What?" He looked at me, a seductive glint in his eyes, and I just shook my head.

"Don't tease me. Please, Brody, don't tease me. I just need to feel you inside me."

"Beg me for it," he said.

"I'm not going to." I cried out as he slid his head inside me. I waited for him to thrust into me completely, but he didn't. He bit down on his lower lip as he stared at me.

"I could be here all day and all night," he said.

"Brody, just fuck me already," I said, grabbing him and pulling him down on top of me.

He chuckled as he kissed me hard, and then I felt him thrusting inside me. He moved fast, and I wrapped my legs around him, loving the way he slid so deep inside me. Loving the way he knew exactly how to hit it. He kissed the side of my neck, and I cried out as his teeth bit down on my skin. And then I felt his fingers on my breasts, and I purred, almost like a cat, as his fingers played with my nipples.

"I love the noises you make. I love to hear you. I love to smell you. I love—oh shit." He pulled out of me quickly and then grabbed my legs and put them over his shoulders before sliding back into me again. He moved quicker this time, his balls bouncing against the underside of my ass as he slammed into me hard and fast. This was primal. This was real. This was as hot as all the other times. And as I felt myself coming, I screamed, not caring that I was being loud or that my body was making noises I'd never known existed before. He grunted before he slammed into me one last time, and I felt him coming inside me before he stilled and dropped back down onto the bed. He was still inside me. And I looked in his eyes as he stroked my face. He kissed me tenderly.

"So, Susie, I have something to ask you."

"Yeah?"

"Do I need to be looking for a nursery in my new house?"

"Sorry, what?" I blinked at him. "Are you trying to tell me you've knocked up some woman?

"No, I'm asking if..." He looked at me and then slid his cock out of me.

We both looked down, and I started laughing. "Oh," I said and shook my head. "No, we're okay."

"Okay," he said. "Because honestly, I wouldn't mind. Honestly, you're the sort of woman that I'd love to have a kid with."

"I think we're going to have to talk about when that moment would be, Brody. I don't even really have a job yet, let alone am I ready to have a baby."

"I know. I'm not ready either. I want years of being with you and fucking you and making you mine before we bring another little Susie into the world. Or a little Brody."

"Oh my gosh." I shuddered. "I can't imagine what it would be like to have a little Brody."

"What does that mean? You know you'd love it."

"I love you, yes. And I would love any children that we had." I groaned. "Oh my gosh, how are we even having this conversation?"

"I don't know." He laughed. "Maybe because I've come inside of you three times, and knowing me, I'd have very potent sperm."

"Okay, well." I paused and chewed on my lower lip. All of a sudden, I was feeling slightly jealous.

"What is it? Why do you look so upset? Why do you look like you shut down?"

"I was just wondering if you've gotten any other women pregnant."

"Honestly?" He looked at me. "And I know you might find this hard to believe, because I would probably find this hard to believe, but you're the only woman I've never used protection with."

"Get out of town, Brody Wainwright." I started laughing. "Seriously?"

"Seriously." He nodded. "Obviously, I haven't been a saint, and obviously, I've gotten around."

"I know, I know. You don't have to tell me more."

"But I've been very careful. Those other interactions were all about just getting some, you know? And this was more about being with the woman I love, and I have to admit that there's something different about making love."

"Oh yeah? You think it's better than fucking?"

"Nothing beats deep, raw fucking, but I think we made love *and* we fucked, right?"

"That does not sound romantic, Brody."

"Well, you're going to have to forgive me because I'm kind of new to this romance thing. However, I do want to get it right."

"It's okay. At least I know whatever you say is sincere."

"I'm nothing if not sincere, my dear."

"Really, Brody?"

"Really." He kissed me on the lips again. "So you'll come with me tomorrow?"

"Sure," I said.

"And you'll think about moving in with me?"

"It's way too soon for us to even talk about that."

"Okay, I get it. But I do have one other question for you."

"Yeah?"

"Will you be my girlfriend, Susie Benedict?"

"What?" My jaw dropped as I stared at him. "What are you asking me?"

"You understand English? I think I was pretty clear."

"Um, but..."

"But nothing. Will you be my girlfriend?"

"Are you sure you want to ask me this? Are you—"

"I know this has been like a whirlwind, and I know you're probably still not even sure if you can trust me or what I say or do, and I understand that. And I understand if you need time. But from the first moment we met, from those first few days together, I knew I was with someone special. I never believed in things like soul mates before, but I'm a total believer now. I truly believe you were made for me. And I truly believe I was made for you. And I want you to know that there is no one that could ever take your place. I want to dedicate myself to you and our love, and oh my God." He shook his head, "If anyone ever heard me saying this, they'd think I had some sort of mental health issue. I sound crazy. I totally don't sound like myself."

I started laughing. "Oh, Brody, are you already regretting what you said?"

"Never. This feeling... It's magical and I never want to lose it. You feel like home to me. You feel like family. You feel like everything." He stroked the side of my face and then kissed me softly. "You're the only person that's ever gotten me to open up in my life, and thank you. Thank you for trusting me. Thank you for giving me so many chances. Thank you for being honest with me. Thank you for caring. Thank you for seeing the man I am inside even when I didn't want to see him."

"I know that what we have is special, Brody," I said softly. "I know that I'm falling in love with you, and I know that you're a good guy, but..."

"But what?" he said, worry on his face.

"No." I touched him softly. "I'm definitely going to be your girlfriend." I grinned. "There's no way I'm letting another woman get you."

He started smiling. "So what's the but about?"

"But I think you need to see a therapist," I said softly, wondering how he'd react. He made a face and sighed, but I prodded on. "I'm always here to talk to you, and I'm sure Finn and Marcia are, but we don't necessarily have everything that you need to work through this. I'm not a professional. I don't know how to help you besides listening and being there for you. This guilt isn't just going to go away in a day or a month or maybe even a year. And your coping mechanisms, they're not going to change overnight. And we're going to have arguments, and we're going to fight, and things are going to happen. I don't want you to rush to a bar. I don't want you to rush to flirt."

"I would never cheat on you," he interrupted me, and I shook my head.

"I know you wouldn't cheat on me, but you might still flirt with someone else. You might still ponder the option. And I don't want you getting drunk. Alcohol isn't the way to cope, you understand?"

"I know," he said. He let out a deep sigh and ran his hand through his hair. "I know. And you're right. Actually, I was thinking about that when I was at the bar. Maybe it's time."

"You were? You were thinking about it?"

"Well, when I thought about you and how I stood you up and how I'd hurt you, I realized that I didn't like who I was. I didn't like how I was acting. And I was scared that perhaps I'd lost you forever. I know I need help and need to process this in the right way. So yeah, I'm willing to see a therapist, and I'm going to do it for me. And maybe I'll also check out some AA classes. I don't think I'm an alcoholic, but I don't think it's healthy for me to turn to alcohol when I need to cope." He smiled at me and touched my face. "Are you sure you want to take this on with me? I know it's a lot,

Susie. And you deserve someone that doesn't have demons or issues. Someone that's got their shit together."

"But who really has their shit together? I'm not perfect either. I've got my own issues too."

"You don't strike me as the type to have issues."

"Maybe not as hardcore as yours, but I have insecurities and other things, you know?"

"But we can work on them together. I'll support you in any way you need me to, Susie." He squeezed my hand and then pulled me up into his arms and held me close to him. I felt his hand rubbing my back, and I pressed my lips against his cheek.

"You're an amazing man, Brody Wainwright. Don't you ever forget it, okay?"

"I think having you by my side for the rest of my life will be all the reminder I need that I'm not a completely horrible person. Because someone like you, someone as beautiful, as kind, as compassionate, as generous, and as strong-willed... Well, she wouldn't be with someone like me unless she saw something. So I'm going to make sure that I prove to you every single day that your faith and your trust is worth it. I love you, Susie Benedict. I love you more than I ever thought was possible. And I know we might not have the easiest road ahead, but I know it's going to be the most fun journey and adventure, and I can't wait. I can't wait to see you in a wedding dress one day while I'm at the end of the aisle waiting for you."

"Brody Wainwright, you are probably one of the most romantic men I've ever met. Which, if you would've told me when I first met you, I never would've believed."

"I never would've believed it either. So should we call Finn and Marcia and tell them the good news?"

I laughed. "Yeah, perhaps. And then I should tell

Shantal and Lilian as well. They are going to be absolutely flabbergasted."

"I'd like to meet them," he said.

"Really?"

"Yeah. Your friends are my friends, and I know they probably don't think the best of me right now. So I want to show them a side of me that is easy to like and love. I want them to be happy for us, for you, for me. I don't want them to think you made a mistake."

"I know. I don't think they will, but it would be helpful if they knew some of the background." I paused. "But obviously if you don't want me to share, I won't."

"No," he said, "you can share. I think one of the biggest problems has been that I've kept it to myself, inside and quiet. I can't do that anymore. Patrick deserves more than that. He deserves to have his name spoken. He deserves to be remembered. I fucked up with that. And you know what? I'm going to reach out to Michael. Maybe he'll want to go to therapy as well. I'm going to reach out to my parents. I'd love for you to meet them. I want to make things right. We all need to move on. We all need to grow. And that's what family is about—forgiveness and love. You made me realize that. I love you."

"I love you too, Brody. More than you'll ever, ever know."

Thank you for reading P.S. Not If You Were The Last Man on Earth. You can read a bonus chapter here.

The next book in the series is P.S. Lose This Number and it is Lilian's book.

To The Guy at The Coffee Shop,

I did not intend to give you my phone number. I was actually waiting on several dates to show up; don't ask, it's a long story. I certainly didn't need to slip my number into your pastry bag just so I could attempt to catch you. I don't even know who you are and I don't care. I found you to be extremely impertinent at the coffee shop. Who interrupts someone else's date to tell their own anecdotes and stories? Especially when that someone else is a stranger. Just because we had a five minute verbal sparring match, it doesn't mean we actually know each other. No, I have no interest in getting dating advice from you. And I certainly have no interest in learning the art of flirtatious touch. Are you out of your mind. All I can say is please stop sending me daily dating tips. Maybe work on not being a cocky ass before you try to help others.

Now Leave Me Alone,

Lilian

P.S. Please Lose This Number

Preorder P.S. Lose This Number now!

ACKNOWLEDGMENTS

First and foremost, I need to thank all of my beta readers Amanda Diaguila Stephens, Teddy, Andrea Robinson, Penny Leidecker, Kelly Gunn, Renee Price, and Lauren Powys. You guys absolutely rock.

Secondly, I have to tell you guys a story. The Half Dome hike story in this book is inspired by my real life experience climbing Half Dome with two guy friends and another girl. She and I were not prepared for the hike at all and we ended up leaving the park around midnight. It was literally a hot mess and I do not recommend to anyone to be like us! :P

Unfortunately, I didn't have a hot guy to massage me and make me feel all better and the end of the hike. The guy I was dating at the time was actually flying over the park with another girl...true story. His scoundrel cheating ways hurt me at the time, but I'm sooooooo happy to have him out of my life now. So always remember that ladies, no matter how much heartbreak and pain a man may put you through, just give it time and be strong enough to break away because I guarantee once you let those assholes out of your life, you will feel a lot better! :) (My Ted talk for the day).

Thanks to all the readers that email, fb message, insta me with comments and love. You guys rock. I love writing, but if no one liked my books or got my humor, it would suck, so here's to those of us who can find the humor, the laughs, and fun in almost every situation. Life is too short to let the little and even the big things get you down!

As always, stay safe, be compassionate, and never give up on love!

Jaimie
XOXO

Made in the USA
Columbia, SC
20 November 2024

46866026R00135